Also by Kate Thompson:

The Switchers Trilogy:
Switchers
Midnight's Choice
Wild Blood
The Switchers Trilogy (3 in 1)

The Missing Link Trilogy
The Missing Link
Only Human
Origins

The Beguilers
(Irish Bisto Award Winner 2002)

The Alchemist's Apprentice
(Irish Bisto Award Winner 2003)

Annan Water
(Irish Bisto Award Winner 2005)

The New Policeman
*(Winner of Guardian Fiction Prize 2005,
Whitbread Children's Book Award 2005 and
Irish Bisto Award 2006)*

The Last of the High Kings

www.katethompson.info

THE FOURTH HORSEMAN

KATE THOMPSON

RED FOX

THE FOURTH HORSEMAN
A RED FOX BOOK 978 0 099 49503 1

First published in Great Britain by The Bodley Head,
an imprint of Random House Children's Books

The Bodley Head edition published 2006
Red Fox edition published 2007

1 3 5 7 9 10 8 6 4 2

Addresses for companies within The Random House Group Limited can be
found at: www.randomhouse.co.uk/offices.htm

Set in Adobe Garamond

Red Fox Books are published by Random House Children's Books,
61–63 Uxbridge Road, London W5 5SA

www.**kids**at**randomhouse**.co.uk

Mixed Sources
Product group from well-managed
forests and other controlled sources
www.fsc.org Cert no. TT-COC-2139
© 1996 Forest Stewardship Council
FSC

THE RANDOM HOUSE GROUP Limited Reg. No. 954009

A CIP catalogue record for this book is available from the British Library.

Printed in the Uk by CPI Bookmarque, Croydon, CR0 4TD

For Mary, Marie-Louise and Caroline

PART ONE

1

When the place filled up with sirens and flashing blue lights I hardly noticed at first. It was just more of the same: chaos upon chaos. I know that what happened took place in broad daylight, but I remember it in darkness. Perhaps I was looking in towards the deep shade beneath the trees. Perhaps it is the other kind of darkness that blackens my memory. We should have been afraid, I suppose, when all those emergency colours came charging in: the blue and red and white. The three of us, anyway: Javed and Alex and I. The 'juveniles'. We could have left Dad to the ambulance crew and made a run for it, vanishing in among the trees. It wouldn't have worked, of course. They would have had the place surrounded and there would have been nowhere for us to go. But none of us even thought of it. We just stood there in an exhausted daze. I suppose it didn't occur to us to feel guilty. We didn't think of what we had done as a crime.

They were upon us within seconds of arriving: two policemen first, then three more, then two sprinting paramedics. I wanted to watch what they did with Dad, but one of the cops was shouting at me.

'Is there anyone in the building?'

I shook my head.

'Are you sure?'

'Positive,' I said.

He turned and called out the information to the others, one of whom was gently but firmly pulling Alex away from Dad so the ambulance crew could work on him. Two others were edging Javed away, out of earshot of the rest of us. We were being quietly separated from each other but it didn't seem important. The horsemen had gone. That was what mattered.

'What happened here?' said the policeman. We were standing beneath the scrubby trees, both of us watching the ambulance crew attending to Dad. I wanted to answer but I didn't know where to start. That was when the first little chemical twinge of anxiety arose. We weren't criminals, we were heroes. It had taken all our courage to do what we did and it was the only thing we could have done, given the circumstances. But how could I even begin to explain?

The policeman moved in front of me, blocking my view of Dad. 'Hmm?' he said. 'What happened?'

That small anxiety became a hot charge of fear. There was no way anyone, let alone the authorities, was going to believe me if I told them the truth about what I had lived through that morning. My silence lengthened, and I knew that the longer it lasted the guiltier I appeared. The policeman was about to speak again, when a red squirrel dropped from a branch above him and landed on his shoulder. He flinched violently and swiped at it with his opposite hand. It dodged the blow and took refuge beneath his arm. As he stood, panic-stricken, trying to work out where it was, I stepped forward and took it off him.

'What the hell . . .?' he said.

I held the squirrel against my chest and stroked her neck. She nuzzled gratefully against me, glad to be back in human hands following her brief glimpse of the free world with its deep dark woods and its huge white sky. She had answered my question and I was about to open my mouth and tell the policeman that this was what it was all about. Little red squirrels. But that wasn't the truth. Not the whole truth, anyway. The whole truth hit me like a furnace blast, and I was suddenly crying, holding the little creature against my neck and face, wetting her shiny red coat with my tears.

2

Lately I have found myself wondering how many, out of all the millions of people out there, have secrets. I don't mean the normal, run-of-the-mill family kind of stuff. I'm sure most people have that kind of secret. What I'm wondering about is the weirder stuff; things that people see or hear but can't tell anyone about because there's no point. No one would believe them. Things from other worlds, other times, other dimensions. Maybe everybody sees things and nobody dares to tell anyone for fear of being ridiculed, so everyone lives a kind of double life, one part private and the other one public. I don't know. But I saw things that I couldn't tell people about. Not many people, anyway, and certainly not the police.

My father saw them too.

He's James McAllister, a well-respected expert on viruses. He studied at various universities until he got his PhD, and then he got a grant from the government to do research at the University of Birmingham on the problem of the New Zealand flatworm.

I know. Everyone laughs when they hear that. But at the time my dad got the project grant it looked as though the New Zealand flatworm was going to become a very serious problem indeed. It arrived in the root balls of imported plants and before very long it was multiplying in the fields and gardens of England. It's a nasty piece of work, the New Zealand flatworm. Dad took me and Alex into the lab to see some of them. They're kind of purply-red and slimy – they look like long strips of liver. The problem with them, and the reason Dad got a grant to try and get rid of them, is that they eat earthworms. They wrap them up and squeeze them, and digest them outside their bodies, then drink up the juice with their sucker mouth. It's pretty gruesome. The problem, as any gardener will tell you, is that earthworms are vital to the health and fertility of the soil, so there was a bad scare when the flatworms were found to be spreading, because there was a danger that they would make the whole countryside barren and useless for growing anything in.

Dad's job was to create a virus that would kill them but wouldn't harm any of the common varieties of earthworm. Dad was certain that it could be done and he wasn't far from creating a preliminary, experimental virus when the money ran out. The New Zealand flatworm suddenly ceased to be an issue. It was still there, still spreading, still dissolving our earthworms, but it hadn't had the rapid, devastating effect that the horticulturists had feared. There were new issues, new scares, and no money left for Dad's project.

He was gutted. The university gave him as much teaching as he wanted, but teaching would never satisfy

Dad. His mind was hungry for research. He wanted to go beyond the explored world and into the unknown. Mum said that he had a pioneering nature, and that it was his best and his worst characteristic. He would never be satisfied with small challenges. He always had to go for the big ones.

My father saw what I saw, though he would never admit to anyone that he did. Being a scientist, he always taught us not to believe anything that couldn't be tested and proved. He said that life was full of rumours and conjectures and wild theories. He said the human race didn't have the mental capacity to grasp the truly miraculous nature of the universe they inhabited, so they invented all kinds of wacky theories to explain it to themselves. He taught us to think straight and work out problems according to the basic principles of science. It's been useful and I'll always be grateful to him, but sometimes thinking straight isn't what's needed. Sometimes you have to think around corners.

Luckily for everyone, just in the nick of time, one of us did.

3

Someone must have told the police what we had done. Dad? He was sitting up now, his head between his knees. A spotless white blanket was around his shoulders, and one of the paramedics was swabbing at the hair on the back of his head. I doubted whether he would have said anything. I doubted whether he even knew what was happening.

Javed must have told them then, or Alex, who was standing watching the paramedic. There was a police constable beside him, watching him carefully. Whoever let it slip, the result was the same. The man who was with me turned and talked to another officer – his senior, I presumed – who had just come over from looking at the building. When he turned back to me his attitude had changed completely. He was no longer embarrassed by my tears, which were drying up now in any case, and he was no longer treading carefully. He was all business, and I was clearly in trouble.

He asked me my name and address and I gave them to him. Then he said: 'You do not have to say anything unless you wish to do so, but it may harm your defence if you do not mention, when questioned, something you may later rely on in court. Anything you say may be given in evidence. Do you understand?'

'In court?' I said. 'Are you arresting me?'

'Do you understand the caution I just gave you?' said the policeman.

'Yes, but you can't arrest me. I've just—'

'Just what?' he said.

Another officer, a woman, appeared at his side. I decided it was probably best not to say anything else. I needed to get things clear in my own mind before I could begin to explain them to anyone else.

'Are we taking her in?' asked the woman.

'That's what I'm told,' said the man. 'I've cautioned her and she says she understands.'

'What are you doing with that?' she asked me, looking at the squirrel.

'Damn thing jumped on me,' said the policeman. 'Gave me the fright of my life.' Turning back to me, he went on: 'You can put it down now. Come on.'

I didn't mind going with them but I didn't want to put the squirrel down. If I let her go again she might not survive. I wished I had thought about that before I turned them all loose.

'Why is it so tame?' asked the female officer. 'Is it a pet?'

I shook my head. 'Not a pet.'

'What then?'

I looked back at the burning building. The wind was blowing the smoke away from us. A great black river of it flowed across the cloudy sky. 'Do you know what went on in there?'

She shook her head and waited, but I wasn't ready to start talking yet.

'Come on,' said the policeman. 'Let's go. Put the squirrel down.'

I put her up instead of down, back on the branch she had jumped from. She scooted away, tail in the air, and disappeared among the shadows. I fought back a fresh crop of tears and sent a little pulse of hope after her. A prayer, I suppose most people would call it.

'Just empty your pockets for me now,' said the woman.

I hesitated, hardly able to believe this was happening. It should have been all over. I was angry and humiliated and frightened. I was sure that my face must be red; shining like a new cricket ball. Reluctantly I emptied my pockets and handed the contents to the officer.

Funny, the things that come into your head; the automatic priorities of the unconscious mind. *Not a tampon* is what I was thinking. *Please let there not be any tampons in my pockets.*

There weren't. What was in there was worse. As I handed each thing to her she examined it then dropped it into the evidence bag her colleague was holding open. A handful of tiny ear tags. The entry card to the lab. A cigarette lighter.

All the proof they needed to convict me.

4

So Dad lost his job and, as far as he was concerned anyway, his career was going down the drain. But ironically, a few months later, Mum's took off. She's a sports physiotherapist, which means she treats all the bumps and breaks and sprains and strains that happen to sports people. She was a great cricketer in her younger days. Before we came along she had played for the England women's team for a couple of seasons, so when the Worcestershire County Cricket Club needed a new physio she was an obvious choice for the job. It suited everyone. Mum was happy because she enjoyed the job. We were happy, because she was nearly always at home when we got back from school. The club was happy because she was very good indeed at what she she did. Which is why, when a sudden vacancy occurred for a physio to work with the England squad, Mum was offered the job. It was a fantastic opportunity for her; a once-in-a-lifetime chance. She wanted it.

But Dad wasn't so keen. They had a big flare-up one night, the worst ever, I think. I couldn't hear what was said, but I could hear the raised voices, the chairs scraping and doors banging, the ominous silences between rounds. Alex came to my bedroom and we rode it out together, listening to music and reading junk magazines and pretending nothing was happening. In the end the row blew itself out, and in the morning Mum was bright and breezy. Dad was a bit more subdued, but they told us with a unified front that Mum was going to be taking the job with the England squad, and that Dad was going to arrange his teaching schedule around our school hours.

'We don't need baby-sitting,' Alex said.

I agreed. 'We can take care of ourselves.' I had my arm in a sling at the time, which made that statement slightly unconvincing, but it was, in fact, quite true. Alex and I were extremely independent. We rode our bikes everywhere and we were well able to cook and clean up after ourselves.

'It's a done deal,' said Dad. 'For the time being, anyway. It's not a problem.'

'If your Dad gets a new research project we might have to rethink,' Mum said, 'but for the moment he'll be holding the fort.'

Dad crossed his eyes and grinned and looked down the barrel of the frying pan. 'Meanwhile, champagne tonight!' He raised an empty hand. 'Here's to your mum's new job!'

It was all a bit sudden, really. There must have been a crisis in the England squad because they wanted Mum yesterday. The Worcester management were very understanding about it. They didn't hold her to her contract with them, and within a week she was gone, off to her new life. We were left slightly dazed, wandering around the empty space that she had left behind her. None of us had realized just how enormous it was going to be.

Dad did his best. There's no doubt about that. While my arm was still in plaster he collected us from school every day, and even when I was able to cycle again he was nearly always there when we got home. If he couldn't be he always let us know and made sure we were organized. He did all his usual absent-minded scientist things, like wearing different-coloured socks and picking us up from school one rainy afternoon in his dressing gown. He used to help us with our homework, and once, when he had been writing out a load of magic formulas to help me with my physics classes, he took them into college instead of his latest lecture notes. At the weekends he took us shopping, or to the cinema, or he bowled a few overs with us at home. Whatever happened he put a brave face on it, but underneath it he was deeply unhappy. I could tell.

There was one particular morning I remember. I was in a miserable mood because I had a sore throat and didn't want to go to school. We had all got up late, and Dad was loading the dishwasher because no one had got around to doing it the night before. Our dog, Randall, was whining for a walk which, that morning at least, he wasn't going to get, and Alex was complaining that his school shirts hadn't been ironed. As Dad straightened up from the dishwasher the spray arm caught in his shirt cuff and the top tray got dislodged. There was an almighty crash of crockery and cutlery, and Dad stood staring at it in disbelief.

'I wasn't born for this,' he said.

'What were you born for then?' said Alex, tactlessly, I thought.

Dad, recovering his sense of humour somehow, laughed, slightly manically. 'Great things, boy,' he said. 'Monumental discoveries.' With sudden and surprising strength he wrenched the dishwasher tray free and plonked it noisily on the worktop. 'I was born to rattle the world in its cage,' he said melodramatically. 'I was born to tilt it on its axis! I was born to stride it like a colossus! The mind' – he pointed to his temple – 'it's all in there.'

We left the havoc in the kitchen and piled into the car, and Dad was in great humour as he drove us to school. But those words of his would return, later, to haunt me.

5

I stared, without focus, into the trees. Specks of soot and flakes of ash were sailing through all the open spaces and coming to rest silently on the rough ground. I watched them as the female officer counted the ear tags she had taken from my pocket.

'Eleven,' she said to the other constable, and then, to me: 'What are these things, anyway?'

'Ear tags,' I said.

'Ear tags,' she repeated. 'For what?'

'Squirrels,' I said.

'Squirrels,' she repeated.

There wasn't going to be any point in lying about that. But how much more would I tell them, that was the question. Javed would know. If they took us in together I would let him do the talking. I looked across to where he too was being searched. As if he had been waiting for me to do that, he caught my eye and held it for a moment. He lifted his hand to his mouth, as though to cover a cough, and then, inconspicuously, altered the shape of it until he had one finger clearly placed across his lips in an ancient and universal sign. Say nothing. I gave a tiny nod, just as inconspicuous, I hoped. He turned his attention back to the officers and their search. They wouldn't find anything incriminating on him, I was pretty sure.

Everything of that nature was on me. I hoped he would let me take the blame. I wished there was a sign I could give him that would say as much, but if there was, I'd never seen it. His position was much more dangerous than mine. The police could make things very difficult for him, especially considering the situation with his father.

It was all so complicated. I looked over at Dad, in the sudden spontaneous hope that he would be better, and would explain it all to the police and take us all home. But the ambulance crew were settling him carefully on to a stretcher. A few metres away Alex was standing between two more of the policemen. My heart lurched when I realized that he was still in his pyjamas; the ones with the legs that were too short for him. He looked suddenly small and vulnerable. I think that upset me more than anything else, the idea that they might be unkind to my little brother. I couldn't bear the thought of him being pushed around, and I took an involuntary step towards him.

The constable put a hand on my arm. 'This way,' she said, pointing with her chin towards the little huddle of waiting squad cars. 'You're going to the police station.' She showed me her badge. 'My name is PC Courtney. I'll be coming with you.'

The stretcher was being lifted and carried towards the ambulance.

'One of us should go with my dad,' I said.

'Don't you worry about your dad,' she said. 'He's going to be fine.' She directed me to the car and protected my head with her hand as I got in. I thought they'd bring the others then, but they didn't. The constable sat in the back with me and slammed the door behind her. The car smelled of disinfectant. Its light was still flashing, but as the driver pulled out into the quiet lane, he switched it off.

Just pulling in to the edge of the road beside the gates was a dark green car. There were two men in the front seats, watching the fire engines fighting the blaze. When he saw us coming, the man in the passenger seat raised a hand to his face, concealing it in the act of putting on a pair of sunglasses. But I knew who he was.

'That's the man you should be arresting,' I said to PC Courtney. 'He's the mastermind.'

I regretted the stupid word as soon as it came out of my mouth.

'Who is he then, this "mastermind"?' she said.

I twisted in the seat and looked back. We were already past and accelerating along the narrow road but I saw the car pulling away rapidly.

'GD zero-eight MFT,' I said. 'At least take down the number.'

'Don't you worry about it,' said PC Courtney. 'We'll find him if we need to.'

But the more I thought about it, the more certain I became that they wouldn't. In fact, there was little or no chance that any of us would be seeing Mr Davenport again.

6

I broke my elbow playing cricket, not long before Mum got offered the new job. It wasn't surprising, given my family history, that I was one of the best young cricketers around. I'd played on the village junior team since I was eleven, and a year later I was asked to start training with the county junior women's team. Bowling was my speciality. I was a leg spinner and had already developed a pretty good 'wrong 'un', so I took plenty of wickets. But I wanted to be an all-rounder, and my batting left a lot to be desired. Mum was always on at me.

'Watch the ball. Watch it right on to the bat. Don't take your eyes off it.'

I tried, and it was beginning to work. Slowly but surely my batting was improving. Until it stopped.

I was thirteen when it happened and I was the youngest player that year to be picked for the under-fifteens first eleven. We were playing a warm-up match against the boys' team when the accident happened. They had batted first and we were chasing a fairly moderate score. I had taken four wickets earlier and my confidence was high. Now, batting at number seven, I knew I could win the match for our side if I could get my eye in and stay at the crease. I defended solidly, giving myself plenty of time to get comfortable. And then, without really thinking about it, I started playing shots. For a few glorious minutes I knew what it felt like to be a batsman. I played drives, cuts, sweeps, the lot. In the space of twenty minutes I scored twenty-five runs, including four fours. My team was getting closer and closer to victory.

The boys didn't like it. Their captain put on their fastest bowler. It wasn't legal to bowl bouncers in our matches, but he bowled one anyway. Afterwards he said he'd just released the ball a bit late and that he hadn't intended to do it, but I saw his face as he ran up to bowl. He meant it. And I got it wrong. All I had to do was watch it. If I'd kept my eye on it I could easily have swerved out of its path. I didn't, though. I panicked. I turned away from it and raised my bat, almost behind me, and the unwatched ball smashed straight into my left elbow.

It felt like a small explosion. For a moment I stood still, too shocked to move. The others on the team said I was as white as my clothes. Then the pain piled in, and I dropped to the ground.

The rest of the story smells of hospitals. I had two operations to gather up the shattered bones and pin them together. Mum gave me exercises, even while I was still in plaster, and hounded me to make sure that I did them.

I did and I didn't. When Mum was there I did. When she wasn't I didn't. But I made a pretty rapid recovery anyway, and the doctors were pleased. The following summer they took the pins out and said I was ready to go back to the cricket pitch. Trouble was, I didn't want to go.

The sports teams were where my friends were, and since my injury had kept me out of the school hockey squad the previous year as well as the cricket, my social life had completely collapsed. I knew, without a shadow of doubt, that I needed to get back on to the pitch and get my life back on the rails, but I couldn't do it. Looking back on it now, I see that I must have been in a depression, just like Dad. I had felt sorry for myself with my broken arm and my ruined social life, and now that I had a chance to fix it, some part of me didn't really want to. I was stuck. I preferred the simplicity of self-pity to the challenges of life. It was easier to stay out of the loop than to face up to my fears on the cricket pitch.

Mum made it worse. By this stage she had been working with the England squad for a year, and she got a month's break at the beginning of the summer, before the season hotted up. As far as I can remember she used the whole month to nag me about going back to the club. The only effect that had was to make me more determined than ever not to go. I did, though, consent to playing a few matches at home, and it was on one of those days that Mum and Alex and I learned about the change in Dad's fortunes.

You might think that four people don't make much of a cricket match and you might be right. But we have a secret weapon: an all-purpose fielder who plays for both sides. He is half Alsatian, half mistake, and his name is Randall. He was called something else, I can't remember what, when we first got him as a pup. But when his particular genius became apparent, Mum decided he should be named after the best fielder she had ever seen, and that was Derek Randall.

If there's anything behind the theory of re-incarnation then Randall was a great cricketer in a former life. For some reason that we have never understood he refuses to retrieve any ball that goes behind the stumps, so one of the fielding team always has to keep wicket. But Randall is perfectly happy to cover the whole of the rest of the pitch and will even go after the fours and sixes that regularly vanish into the undergrowth at the edges of the field. When the bowler is running up Randall takes up position at mid-on, watching the batsman like a hawk. We play with a regulation ICC hard ball, but Randall has no fear of it. He has taken some spectacular, jaw-crunching catches in his time and has never seemed any the worse for it. The best thing about him though, and the thing that makes me think he must be the smartest dog in England, is that he always, always, always takes the ball back to the bowler. Even if it's a stranger, someone he's never met before, he remembers who's bowling and delivers the ball straight to their feet. There's a dark side to everything, as Mum often says, and the price we have to pay for Randall's participation is the slimy dog drool that he leaves on the ball. We have to wipe it off on the grass before we polish the ball on our trousers, and some visitors find it a bit distasteful. But we think it's a small price to pay. Without Randall we just couldn't have had those small, two-a-side matches.

He was in particularly good form that day, delighted to have the family back together again and doing what, in his view at least, we had been put on earth to do. But Dad played disastrously, missing catches, misjudging his line and length, losing wicket after wicket (we all had to bat several times each) through sheer carelessness. He was so cheerful that we thought he was doing it on purpose, but he wasn't. It was just that he had something else on his mind. When it started drizzling he tore up the stumps and led the way back to the house in a triumphant sort of way, even though he and I had lost the match by about thirty-five runs. It wasn't until the kettle was on and we were all gathered round the table helping ourselves to sandwiches that we found out what was bothering him. That was when he told us there was something he wanted to talk to us about. That was when we first heard Mr Davenport's name.

7

I watched out of the window of the squad car as we drove along the quiet lanes. We were only about four miles from the house where I had lived all my life, but until a year or so ago I hadn't known the area existed. There were very few buildings, just the occasional farmhouse and yard. There were meadows and cornfields, but most of the land was covered by orchards. Their days were numbered, Dad had told us, because they didn't produce the kinds of apples that the EU wanted. Some of them were being grubbed up already.

'What's all this with the squirrels, anyway?' said PC Courtney.

I didn't answer. I couldn't remember the exact words of the caution I'd been given, but I was pretty sure I didn't have to say anything.

'What was it?' she went on. 'A zoo or something?'

When I still said nothing she talked to the other constable, the man who had cautioned me and who was now driving the car. 'Do you know anything about the place, Chris?'

He shook his head. 'I never even knew it existed. No idea what they were doing there.'

'Squirrels,' said PC Courtney. 'Was there any other kind of animal there?'

'No,' I said, then wished I hadn't. If I was going to say nothing I should say nothing.

'Just squirrels?' she said. 'So why did they have the little ear tags?'

I didn't answer.

'Was there some kind of experimentation going on?'

'Must have been something like that,' said the policeman called Chris. 'Funny we never heard anything about it.'

'Is that what this is all about?' said PC Courtney. 'Are you an animal rights activist or something?'

I kept quiet, and she sighed and gave up questioning me. By now we were approaching the familiar outskirts of Worcester and the car had slowed behind a line of traffic. I realized I knew very little about the law. What did they do with young offenders? I was pretty sure I was too young to go to prison, but I thought they had places where they locked up juveniles. Could I handle that? Would I have to be in there for years?

I wondered if someone would get less time behind bars for being an animal rights activist or more time. I knew the authorities had been getting much tougher on them in recent years. I would have to think about that.

8

Animal rights activists came into our conversation that day after the rained-off match, when Dad broke the news to us about the offer he'd had from Mr Davenport.

We were sitting round the kitchen table drinking tea and eating cucumber sandwiches, which was traditional during our cricket matches. The rain was still falling outside, but Mum was optimistic that it would stop and that we could resume later on.

'It's another government project,' said Dad. 'I was on their records for the flatworm work and so they didn't have to look very far to find me. It's essentially the same kind of project, but this time there's no doubt about the need for it. It's a scheme to save the red squirrel.'

He didn't need to spell out the background to us. We all knew that red squirrels were on the point of being wiped out entirely by the more successful grey ones.

He went on: 'This Davenport bloke says they have no facilities yet but they'll find something nearby if I agree to take it on. They'll start paying me straight away and I can get the theoretical work up and running. Then I can start on the practical side of things when they find a suitable lab.'

'Are there any round here?' I asked.

'They can adapt practically any kind of building apparently,' said Dad. 'Money seems to be no object.'

'So what exactly would you have to do?'

'Well, pretty much what I was doing with the flat-worms. Study the genetic codes and create a virus that will . . .' He hesitated.

'Kill the grey ones,' said Alex.

'Well, yes,' said Dad.

'And not the red ones,' said Alex.

'That's about the size of it, yes.'

We all thought about that for a while, and it was clear that Dad was the only one of us who had any enthusiasm for the idea.

'It seems cruel, I know,' he said eventually. 'But sometimes you have to be cruel to be kind.'

'No you don't,' said Alex. 'All you have to do to be kind is be kind.'

'You know what I mean,' said Dad. 'I don't really like the idea of killing the grey squirrels, but they're killing off the red ones wholesale. If something isn't done about it they'll soon be extinct.'

'In Britain,' said Mum.

'Yes, in Britain. I don't know about other places.'

We still didn't like it. Mum in particular looked very dubious.

'I know what you're thinking,' Dad said to her. 'Myxomatosis.'

She nodded. 'I was, actually, yes.'

We were all familiar with myxomatosis. It was a rabbit disease that had been introduced from South America into Australia a few decades ago to control the expanding rabbit population. Accidentally, they say, it got into the UK as well, and began spreading across the country. Its effects were dreadful. It caused a slow and painful death, and most people who lived in the countryside were familiar with the sight of 'myxie' rabbits, their heads swollen, their closed eyelids bulging. Ironically, Dad had told us about it as an example of how not to use virology in the environment but now, it seemed, he was willing to do something similar himself.

'This will be different,' he said. 'For one thing I'll make sure the virus works rapidly. No long, lingering deaths.'

'Can you do that?' I asked.

'I think so,' said Dad.

'And for another thing?' said Mum, still sounding sceptical.

'For another thing, we won't be introducing it wholesale across the countryside. We'll just give it to the red squirrels and let them pass it on.'

'Oh, great,' said Alex. 'Doesn't that defeat the whole purpose?'

'No,' said Dad. 'Because the red squirrels won't die from it.' I watched his eyes grow bright as he talked.

Dad was not beyond being enthusiastic about other things in life – cricket, for example – but nothing excited him as much as his own field of endeavour. We could all see that he had already become emotionally charged by the possibilities of the new project. 'It'll be like a common cold to them. In fact that's what I'll base the new virus on: some common or garden disease that all squirrels get. But I'll change it, just a bit, so that it's lethal to the greys.'

'How?' said Alex.

'Depends. What I'll need is a small but significant difference in some important cell. I'll have to study the genome analysis of both species and see if I can find something to work on. Mr Davenport says he already has them. There are a couple of companies in America that specialize in producing genome plans from anything you give them. That's why it's all ready to go. I can be working on them while he finds the lab facilities.'

'But why would you want the reds to get it as well?' I asked.

'That's the beauty of it,' said Dad. 'We give it to the red squirrels and they carry it, passing it around among each other the way we pass around a cold. But whenever a grey one comes along he catches it and snuffs it. Hopefully he passes it around to a few mates first, and they snuff it as well. So the red squirrels become more successful, because they can breed and take back the territory they've lost to the grey ones. And the grey ones will just fall back as they advance.

'You see?' He turned to Mum in something close to desperation. He badly needed her blessing. 'It's not like myxomatosis at all. There's no need to infect the whole grey squirrel population. We'll just give the reds a bit of an advantage, that's all. A kind of secret weapon.'

'Was that bit your idea or Mr Davenport's?' I asked.

'Mine,' said Dad. 'But he's delighted with it. Says it's perfect.'

But Mum was still uneasy. 'What bothers me is why all the secrecy? I would have thought that it would be a popular initiative. Wouldn't the government make some political capital out of it if they made it public?'

'They will, later,' said Dad. 'But not until the work is finished, because of the animal rights activists. They're everywhere, in every nook and cranny. I'm going to have to experiment on real squirrels, and you know what some of these people will think of that.'

Mum nodded guardedly.

'They're practically terrorists, some of them,' Dad went on. 'They don't just picket laboratories and write letters to the newspapers any more. They threaten the researchers and their families. Life wouldn't be worth living if any of those fanatics got a whiff of the project. We'd have to barricade ourselves in and take the kids to school in an armoured car.'

'All the more reason not to get involved in the first place, I would have thought,' said Mum.

Dad walked out. He didn't say anything, he just walked out, reaching for his cigarettes as he went. Mum looked miserable. We all knew what was happening.

'He really needs this, Mum,' I said.

'I know he does,' she said.

'And anyway,' I said, 'it all seems a bit unlikely to me. I have a funny feeling nothing will ever come of it even if Dad does agree to do it.'

'Maybe you're right,' she said.

'I am. And you have to support him. He supported you, remember?'

Mum nodded and I knew she had come round. I'd won the day for Dad and I was delighted with myself.

But I wasn't half as clever as I thought I was. Not by a very long chalk.

9

I had passed the front of the police station in Worcester a thousand times but I had never before seen the back of it, and I had never been inside any part of it. I was driven into a kind of yard and from there taken in through a heavy door. It was very quiet inside the building and I was astonished when I caught sight of a clock on the wall and realized what time it was. Still only ten thirty in the morning. The extraordinary, cataclysmic events that had led up to our arrest had all happened in not much more than an hour. I found it almost impossible to believe. It felt more like a week.

There was no sign of the others. They must have left a while after we did, but I presumed they would appear before too long. I was keen to see both of them, for different reasons. I was worried about Alex.

'Can I see my brother?' I asked PC Courtney.

'Not yet,' she said. 'Don't worry, though. We'll look after him.'

We were standing in a wide corridor beside a closed door. A few metres away the policeman called Chris was talking quietly to another officer who I suspected, from his demeanour rather than his dress, was senior. I couldn't make out much of what they said but I heard the occasional word here and there. 'Eleven what? . . . Squirrels? . . . How old are they?'

PC Courtney must have heard that as well, because she asked me, 'How old are you?'

'Fifteen,' I said, and then, as if it made any difference, 'Nearly sixteen.'

'That man is the custody officer,' she told me. 'His name is Sergeant Woolley. He'll take some details in a minute.'

The other two wound up their conversation and the sergeant opened the door and led us into the room.

'She's fifteen,' PC Courtney told him. 'Laura McAllister with an address in Broadheath.'

'Laurie,' I said. 'Not Laura.'

The sergeant spent a few minutes logging on to a computer, presumably opening a new file. He asked me to spell my name, and typed it in.

'Date of birth?'

I told him and he typed that in as well. Then he turned to PC Courtney, who launched into a long-winded description.

'There has been a fire at a building in Hetherington Lane causing a high degree of damage, and this person was found close by. We can't tell yet whether or not the fire was started deliberately but this person was found to be in possession of certain items, including an entry card, believed to be for access to the building, and a cigarette lighter, which led me to believe that the fire was started deliberately, and that this person is one of those responsible for causing the fire. She was arrested at the scene and brought straight here.'

She handed over the bag with the contents of my pockets in it and the sergeant wrote something on it in black marker, and then typed something else into the computer. Then he asked me whether I was hurt, or whether I had any illnesses or disabilities, or whether I was on any kind of medication. I answered no to everything.

'You'll need to call an appropriate adult to be with you when we question you,' said Sergeant Woolley. 'I understand your father has been taken to the hospital.'

'Yes,' I said. 'Have you heard anything?'

'Not yet. We'll make enquiries and let you know as soon as we can. What about your mother? Should we call her?'

I shook my head. There was no one on earth I would rather have seen at that moment than my mother. But she, as luck would have it, was about as far away as it was possible for her to be, happily ignorant of the storm that surrounded the rest of us. She was at a conference way down under, in the home of the notorious flatworm.

🙞 10 🙜

Dad took the job, inevitably, but it took some time for all the details to be worked out and it wasn't until August that he went to London to meet Mr Davenport and sign a contract. He told us that he had to sign the Official Secrets Act as well. When Mum heard that she went ballistic.

'The Official Secrets Act? I thought only soldiers and spies had to sign that. Since when have squirrels been enemies of the state?'

'It's the animal rights activists again,' said Dad. 'There have been some terrible cases recently. People intimidated, places closed down. They don't want loose talk wasting them a humungous amount of money, that's all.'

'Well, we all know. Did anyone think of that? What happens if Laurie or Alex tell their mates?'

'They won't,' said Dad, looking daggers at us.

We wouldn't, of course, but it did all seem a bit sloppy if it was so important.

'Well,' said Mum, 'I just hope you know what you're doing.'

'I know exactly what I'm doing,' said Dad.

Within a few days of Dad signing the contract, a courier arrived at our house with a fantastic brand-new state-of-the-art computer. He and Dad manhandled the huge box into the study and Alex and I brought in the printer and the scanner and other smaller things. One of them was a package containing DVDs, which had the squirrel genome information from the company in the USA.

For the next couple of days Dad immersed himself in the study, feverishly clearing out all the debris that had gathered there over the last ten years and making a clear space for the launch of his new venture. Alex and I hovered in the wings, carrying out rubbish, helping to move tables and desks from one part of the house to the other as Dad tried to decide what the best arrangement would be. We begged for a go on the new computer but Dad said no. Finally and categorically no. We could use his old computer but the new one – and the study as well for that matter – was completely out of bounds to us and there were to be no exceptions. This job was too important.

We didn't ask Dad how much the government was paying him, but we had the impression that it was a princely wage. He talked about building a chalet in the garden when the mortgage was paid off so he could have a proper study outside in peace and quiet and not be in everybody's way. He put in an order to one of the office supply companies and another courier arrived the next day with four huge boxes. There was a new swivel chair and a smart red filing cabinet. There were thirty reams of paper, a half-dozen printer cartridges, bulk wrapped jotter pads and a gross of ballpoint pens. There was every kind of file, folder and storage box under the sun, in all the colours of the rainbow.

'Are we opening a shop, Dad?' Alex asked.

'Help yourselves,' said Dad, and we did. We were the best supplied students in our school when we started back for the new year the following week. But it didn't do Alex any good. In fact, it might have been one of the reasons that he got into trouble.

I couldn't think of who else to call on as my 'appropriate adult'. Attiya Malik kept coming into my head, but I knew that she would probably be called in to be with Javed, and I doubted that we could share her. We knew loads of people in the area, but I couldn't think of anyone who would be just right. Our nearest neighbours were the Davidsons and I had known them all my life, but they were getting on and they both had medical conditions which wouldn't respond particularly well to the stress of being called into the police station. Mum's parents had moved to Ireland a few years ago, and Dad's were in their house in Spain, where they spent at least half of every year.

'I can't think of anyone,' I told the sergeant.

'There must be someone,' he said.

'I know there must,' I said. 'I just can't think of anyone.'

'We'll have to appoint someone for you then,' he said.

'Who?'

'There are a couple of people on call,' he said. 'Social workers. We'll get one to come in.'

'A social worker?' I didn't like the sound of it. Social workers dealt with neglected kids from council estates, not nice middle-class people like me.

'Unless you can come up with someone else for us.'

I racked my brains, but no one came to mind.

'We'll find someone suitable,' he said. 'Meanwhile you'll have to wait out there.' It was a sign to my keeper that the session was over. She led me back out into the corridor and along to another room.

A juvenile detention room, it was called. To me, when PC Courtney had gone and locked the door behind her, it felt like a cell. It felt like prison.

There was nothing in the room except a table and a couple of hard plastic chairs. Sounds from other parts of the building echoed indistinctly through the bare walls. I hated the place but I realized that it was a relief to be alone; to have a chance for the first time that dreadful morning to think. I sat down on a chair and sprawled across the table. My head felt heavy and I rested it on my arms. I wanted to sleep, but I knew it would be a long, long time before I could expect to get that kind of release.

⇥ 12 ⇤

They say that every cloud has a silver lining, but I never knew what that meant until Alex got beaten up on the way home from school.

Mum was at home again for a couple of weeks that September because the summer season had ended and there was a break before the team embarked on the first of that year's winter tours. Dad was practically invisible, working frenetically on the squirrel genomes, living in the stuffy study during daylight hours, emerging only for coffee or the odd weekend cricket match. Alex and I were about three weeks into the term, when he came home black and blue.

Normally we cycled together, but that day his class had been on a trip to an archaeological dig so he'd come home late, on his own. At first he insisted that he had come off his bike. Mum didn't believe it. She wasn't exactly a forensics expert but she did know a lot about injuries and she was as sure as she could be that Alex's hadn't come from a fall. Eventually he admitted that he'd been in a fight, but he said he didn't know the boys who had done it. He said they had jumped him from the side of the road when he was taking the short cut through the back streets. But he refused to tell anyone exactly where it had happened and he wouldn't let Dad call the police. He stayed at home for a couple of days hoping that the bruises would disappear, but of course they just got blacker. On the third day he came down to breakfast with the local newspaper under his arm.

'I want to learn martial arts,' he said.

'What, karate and stuff?' I said.

'Sounds like a good idea,' said Mum. Alex wasn't all that short but he was as skinny as a whippet and I knew Mum worried about him. She was always trying to feed him, a tactic which backfired consistently because of Alex's contrary temperament.

'Not karate,' he said. 'Aikido.' He showed us a newspaper ad in the paper. The classes were on Saturday mornings at a hall on our side of the town. A new beginners' session was due to start that week.

'Go for it,' said Dad. 'Even if you never need to use it you can't go wrong with that kind of thing. It'll give you great confidence.'

It gave Alex a lot more than that. The aikido class led to him meeting the best friend he had made in his life so far. Javed Malik was the silver lining to that dark cloud. They were the same age and roughly the same height and weight, which is why they were put together as partners in the first class. They clicked instantly, and after the second class they exchanged telephone numbers and arranged to meet during the week. Javed went to a different school but he lived on our side of town and he had a bike as well, so it was easy for the two of them to get together. Alex went to Javed's house first and discovered that they had more than aikido in common. Javed's bedroom walls were papered with posters of cricketers, and he was one of the county's best batsmen in his age group. The next time they met up, Javed came to our house, and for a few weeks that autumn he practically moved in.

We were lucky to live where we did, even though we sometimes grumbled about it being too far from town. My mum's mother had been born in the house and handed it over to my parents when they married, on the condition that they took out a mortgage on it so Mum's parents could buy a house in Ireland. If we'd had to buy it from scratch it would have been way out of our league, not only because the house was large and very desirable, but because it stood on three and a half acres of gardens, orchards and paddocks. We had been given a pony when I was small by Dad's nutcase of a sister, who lived in Scotland. The pony was beautiful to look at and not at all bad for a young child to ride, but it was practically impossible to catch. Faced with that constant frustration, my 'horsy' phase was very short, and we passed the pony on to a nearby riding school for peanuts. He is still there, as far as I knew, and is still practically impossible to catch. As soon as he was gone Mum had his paddock ploughed, re-seeded and rolled into a cricket pitch. From the time I was eight and Alex was six we had been playing family cricket matches.

During the summer we had bigger matches, involving as many friends and neighbours as we could muster, and once a year we had a huge, chaotic match between Mum's team and Dad's team, which was known as the Family Row. Mum invited her old cricketing mates, and Dad had found a few handy players among his friends and colleagues as well. There was no limit to the number of people who could play, so we invited friends, cousins, neighbours, schoolfriends – anyone who would come. The only real rule of the Family Row was that neither side was allowed to win, so it was a real fun occasion. It went on for two days, and in the evenings we had parties. It was one of the highlights of every summer.

When Javed first saw our pitch he looked as if all his birthdays had come at once. We'd had some rain and the outfield was a bit soggy, but we played a short match just so he could have a taste of it. Mum was well impressed with his batting. She told me later that she could see him going a long, long way. There was room for improvement in his technique, she said, but his strength was that he watched the ball right on to the face of the bat. She didn't say any more. She was, as ever, tactful about the accident that had broken my elbow, and the reason it had happened. But I did ask Javed once, a while later, what his secret was and he told me with no hesitation.

'The first part is waiting,' he said. 'My father told

me there's only one ball in a game of cricket and that's the one you're facing. It doesn't matter what has happened in the past. The ball that's coming at you won't be like the last one or the next one, so you don't predict. You wait and see, and you don't make any decisions until it has left the bowler's hand. If you can, you even wait until it has hit the pitch. Then you decide what to do.'

'No one can think that fast,' I said.

'That's the other bit of the secret,' he said. 'Don't think. Act. If you start thinking you've had it, because you're right, no one can think that fast.'

I thought about it and I had to admit it made some sort of sense. The best catches I ever took were ones that came too fast for me to think about.

'But how do you stop yourself thinking?' I said.

Javed shrugged. 'That's what I'm trying to find out,' he said. 'That's why I'm learning aikido.'

⚜ 13 ⚜

That room, or cell, was strangely peaceful. It felt like a refuge from the madness. There were too many things in my mind that I didn't want to think about. The lab and all that went on there, the squirrels, dead and living, my father in hospital, my brother in custody, and beyond all that the perilous state the world was in. Over every thought and feeling loomed the dreadful figures of the horsemen, colouring everything else that had happened and might happen. It was all too much.

It was only the thought of Javed that comforted me. I don't know why I trusted him as much as I did. I'd always liked him but it wasn't until this morning that I had developed such a huge respect for him. I would accept his judgement now without question. After all, he was the one who had figured out what was going on. He was the one who could think around corners. He had advised me to say nothing, and that was what I would do, at least for the moment. And I would wait, like a batsman at the crease, for the next ball to arrive.

PART TWO

PART TWO

1

It was nearly a year after Alex met Javed when Dad and I saw the first of the riders. It was early the following summer, and it was the day the squirrels arrived.

Dad had been in great spirits since he started on the new research. He had devised a programme that compared the squirrel genomes with the human one, which had already been analysed and recorded. A huge percentage of human genes are shared with other animal species, but Dad wasn't interested in those. Any gene sequence that was the same in both human and squirrel genomes was discarded, so all that was left at the end were the genes that were peculiar to the squirrels. He then ran the red and the grey side by side through the programme, and it eliminated all the squirrel genes that they had in common. What was left at the end was the differences. There was still a phenomenal amount of information there for him to analyse, but it was a lot easier to manage in its reduced state.

His only worry was that for nearly a year after he started work there was no concrete evidence of an actual lab for him to use for the practical side of the project. He found it very hard to get in touch with Mr Davenport, who didn't appear to have a regular office but operated on a system of perpetually changing mobile phone numbers. Whenever he did succeed in contacting him he was always given the same story: it was progressing well and there was no need to worry about it. No matter how hard Dad pressed him, Davenport refused to give any details about where the lab would be, and Dad eventually came to believe that there never would be a lab, and that the whole project would disappear as suddenly and as finally as the flatworm one. But he was wrong. One day, out of the blue, Davenport arrived in a Mercedes and took Dad away to see the new complex. When he came back we were all amazed and delighted to learn that it was only about four miles away. Dad had been afraid that it might be in another county somewhere and that he'd be faced with logistical problems about Alex and me. As it was, with the lab so close, he could still be here when we came home from school, and if he needed to put in more hours he could start early in the mornings or go back to work in the evenings. As far as Mr Davenport was concerned it was entirely up to him. He had confidence in Dad's integrity and no one was counting the hours he put in. What most people wouldn't give for a boss like that, eh? That's what we thought too.

The only time I ever met him was the day he came to take Dad to the lab. When they came back Dad was beaming all over his face. It was clear he very much liked what he had seen. He went to get some paperwork from his study and Mr Davenport sat down with Alex and me in the kitchen. I can see his face now in my mind's eye and it still gives me the shivers. He was tall and heavily built and he had thinning hair, pepper and salt. He had sunglasses that he never took off, so I couldn't say what colour his eyes were. He had jowls, I remember, like a bulldog. I didn't like him. He frightened me, and Alex as well, I think, telling us how important it was that nobody, not even our best friends, should get to hear about what Dad was doing, and he went on and on about animal rights activists and how dangerous they could be. He spoke to us as if we were mentally deficient, but it was clear that he was doing his best to be nice. It didn't work, though. We just felt threatened.

When Dad came back with the papers, Mr Davenport took them and left immediately, ignoring the offer of tea and sandwiches. The rest of us sat for a long time in a kind of daze, like mice crouching among the weeds long after the shadow of the hawk has gone. It was creepy.

Mr Davenport had insisted that absolutely nothing pertaining to him or to the project should remain at our house once the lab complex was ready. So Dad took Alex and me along to help him move the computer and all the other stuff that had been delivered to the house by the office suppliers. He had to make three trips because there was no way it would all fit in the car.

After a couple of miles we entered a network of tiny, leafy lanes, and it seemed to me so unlikely that there was a lab down there that I began to think Dad was pulling our legs. I had done a lot of cycling on the country roads around Worcester but I'd never discovered this area before. There were very few houses, and those we did see blended into the countryside as though they were still part of it. It felt like a real backwater. Eventually we stopped at a pair of old gates that looked as though they led into the farmyard of some ramshackle old estate. Which was, in fact, exactly what they did. Now we were convinced that Dad was having us on, and Alex told him so. The gates looked as if it would take a weight-lifter to open them, but Dad showed us the keypad ingeniously concealed in an old wooden post beside the entrance. He punched in the number and the huge gates swung open on oiled hinges and then closed silently behind us. Round the corner of the gravelled driveway was a range of old brick outbuildings. The ones at the front were decaying, their slate roofs collapsing and their windows fallen out. Inside them old wooden mangers dangled from rusting nails and the black sludge of ancient manure covered the floors. But behind them was a second yard and here the buildings were in far better condition.

Dad parked his car round the back, beneath the cover of an old Dutch barn. It was hidden there and wouldn't be seen by anyone if they came snooping around. We walked back to the better of the two yards. The windows and most of the doors were firmly boarded up. The buildings still looked like farm out-houses, but in the dark corner of a lean-to hayshed was a discreet but very solid wooden door, and beside it, blending ingeniously into the brickwork, was a card slot and a fingerprint recognition pad.

Inside, there was a whole complex of rooms. The first one was huge; a long hall lined with sturdy metal cages, ready and waiting for the arrival of the squirrels. Beyond that was an office, which was where the computer and all the other stuff was going to go, and beside it a kitchen and a bathroom. None of the rooms had any natural light because windows, even skylights, would allow a curious passer-by to look in and they had all been boarded up. So once you were inside you might have been anywhere. The walls were freshly painted and plasterboard ceilings concealed the wooden beams of the old buildings. The built-in desks and work units were brand new and the whole place was clean and sparkling. Further on again we came to the quarantine room with its showers and de-contamination chambers. Only one of its doors would open at a time, which meant that you couldn't accidentally leave a passage through which a virus could escape. Everything that passed in or out of the virology lab had to be sterilized or quarantined in a special sealed box. Even people had to be scrubbed, on the way in as well as on the way out, and that was why Dad didn't take us any further that day. It would take too long for everyone to shower and change, he said, and there wasn't much to see in there anyway. The inner lab was a sealed chamber containing the machines and chemicals he needed to test blood and to isolate, identify and manipulate viruses. There was a second computer in there, and all manner of specialist equipment. There was another tiny kitchen and bathroom area as well, where he could smoke well away from the sensitive machinery, and a sealed room where the virus would actually be tested on the animals. There was an incinerator built into the outside wall for all the rubbish. It burned with a ferocious heat but it was well insulated, and its flues were lined with filters that prevented anything that might be dangerous from entering the outside air.

'You won't even see smoke when it's operating,' he told us. 'Just a heat shimmer above the chimney.'

It wasn't until we went back out that we realized how truly bizarre the set-up was. Outside was Victorian England, red brick, the remnants of a forgotten kind of agriculture. Inside was cutting-edge genetic engineering.

When we had finished unloading the car Alex and I left Dad to set up the office and went exploring. The yards had once been contained by a low stone wall. In some places it was still standing, but most of it had fallen. Beyond it, and surrounding the whole complex of buildings, was a combination of old woodland and younger scrub. The air in the woods was cool and fresh, the way it always seems to be under old trees, no matter what kind of day it is. Coincidentally, or ironically perhaps, there were squirrels in there. We saw two of them, grey ones, both hurtling through the branches away from us. It was a beautiful, peaceful place, but there was something about it that made me uneasy. I think Alex felt it as well, because he didn't show his usual adventurous spirit. We were both reluctant to go out of sight of the buildings, and we turned back long before we found out how far the woodland went.

I don't know what it was that made us feel like that about the woods. We were country kids, born and bred, and had no fear of the natural world, even in its most quiet and ancient places. Thinking back, I wonder whether we had some kind of premonition of what was going to come. Maybe the horsemen were already there, watching us from the deep, cool shadows, seen only by the curious squirrels.

2

About a fortnight later the squirrels were delivered to the lab. Dad had gone there early on a Saturday morning to take charge of them and I was still in bed when he phoned me. I had nothing in particular to do that day and I was luxuriating in the lie-in.

'I need a hand,' said Dad. 'I can't manage them on my own.'

'Manage what?' I said, trying my best not to sound grumpy.

'The squirrels. They're all babies. Tiny little things. They keep biting me.'

I had to laugh at that and it lifted my mood. I promised to come to his rescue as soon as I'd had breakfast. I wasn't sure what I could do to help him, other than get myself bitten instead of him, but I was dying to see the baby squirrels. I gobbled my breakfast while I was getting dressed and ran out to the shed. Alex's bike was gone and I remembered that he was away for the night. Not only had our family adopted Javed, but Javed's family had adopted Alex as well. He had been especially invited by Javed's mum to stay for a day or two because her mother and sister were visiting from Shasakstan and there were going to be all kinds of parties going on.

It took me exactly half an hour to get to the lab on

my bike. I couldn't get in through the gates so I cycled on a bit further to see if there was another way in for someone on foot. There wasn't. An old wall ran along beside the road for about three hundred metres, then turned inland and ran along the side of a cornfield. It was a good two and a half metres high at its lowest point and impossible to see over. On the other side of it was the woodland Alex and I had begun to explore a couple of weeks ago. I couldn't tell from there but I guessed that the wall went all the way round the old farm buildings and their woodlands. The top of it was concrete embedded with chunks of glass, their sharp edges pointing upwards, and it looked to me as if some of it had been recently replaced. The lab was clearly well protected.

I went back to the gate and phoned Dad on my mobile to get the numbers for the keypad. 7686. I committed them to memory as I punched them in, then cycled through the open gates and round to the back yard. I wondered who had done the conversion, and how they had managed to keep it quiet. There was no sign of them left behind – no piles of rubble or drifts of plastic and polystyrene. No empty milk cartons or crisp packets lying around. Healthy weeds were growing through the gravel of the drive and between the old paving stones of the yards. It was all just a little bit too perfect, and as I passed beneath the overhanging branches at the edge of the yard I got that uneasy feeling again. Something about this was wrong.

Dad opened the door for me and led the way into the cage room. It was completely silent – no sign of squirrels anywhere. But on the central island where the feed and cleaning tools were kept several square shapes were standing, covered by a dark grey blanket.

'They're in there,' said Dad. He lifted the blanket and all hell broke loose. In six small hamster cages three dozen young squirrels burst into frenzied activity, hurling themselves at the sides and tops of the cages with surprising force.

'Look.' Three of Dad's fingers had plasters on. He pulled one of them off and showed me a tiny wound. 'They're all very cross for some reason.'

'Wouldn't you be?' I said. 'Cooped up like that. Where have they come from?'

'I don't know,' said Dad. 'Mr Davenport said they were bred in captivity but he didn't say where.'

'Who would be breeding squirrels in captivity?' I asked. 'They're not normally used in lab experiments, are they?'

'No,' said Dad. 'And they don't behave like lab mice or rats either. Whoever bred these hasn't tamed them at all.' He waved his bitten fingers again and I laughed.

'I was going to put them into the big cages,' he went on.

'We can just pour them in, can't we?' I said.

'We could, but how would we ever get them out again?'

I could see his point. I didn't have any experience of small animals. Some of my friends kept hamsters or gerbils but I never had.

'I think we should leave them where they are until we can get them used to being handled. There must be a way of doing it.'

'I'll ask around,' I said.

'Carefully,' said Dad.

'Or I might find something on the Internet. Can I use your computer?'

'No,' said Dad. 'Wait until you get home. There's no rush.'

He tipped some hamster food into each of the cages, setting off the panic reactions again. The little creatures were really cute, even if they did bite.

'Can I do it, Dad?' I said. 'Get them used to us, I mean. They're gorgeous. I wouldn't mind coming in and playing with them.'

'That'd be perfect,' he said. 'Are you sure?'

'Definitely.'

'You have a deal,' he said. 'And I might even be able to find a bit of extra pocket money for you.'

We filled all the little dropper bottles with water and left the baby squirrels to themselves for a while. Dad was staying, but he came out into the yard to have a cigarette as I was leaving, and that was when I saw him.

A man dressed in flowing white clothes, astride a white horse, shining in a patch of sunlight beneath the trees. My mind faltered. He couldn't be there, and not only because of the wall and the gates. He couldn't be there because he didn't belong to the world I lived in. He was too big, too bright; like something that had walked out of the world of dreams. But he wasn't a dream. He was there.

I turned to Dad, wondering whether he had seen him too. I don't know which scared me most, the horseman or what I saw on my father's face. I was shocked and frightened but Dad's reaction was entirely different. He was mesmerized. He looked like a sleep-walker, or someone who has been hypnotized. He was staring at the rider with glazed, dreamy eyes, and he was swaying slightly on his feet. I turned back to the horseman, and saw that he was looking directly at Dad. I had the sense of being an observer in an intensely powerful but private meeting. However dreamlike the horseman might appear, the power he had over Dad was real. I might have been a shadow or a photograph for all the significance I had during that exchange.

I don't know how long I stood, paralysed, staring. The horse was beautiful; a gleaming white pin-up of a creature. It was heavy, with big feet and feathered legs, but it wasn't a carthorse. It had a handsome, noble head and soft brown eyes, and it stood quite still, strong and patient. The rider was tall and upright, with a noble bearing. His white robes flowed down over the horse's flanks. Around them both, flies circled in the still air.

It was Dad who broke the long, tense silence. He gave a strange little sigh, or moan, and took a few swaying steps towards the rider under the trees.

'No! Dad!' I acted instinctively, ungluing my feet from the ground and lunging at him, grabbing him round the neck. His eyes opened wide. He looked like someone startled out of a doze in front of the TV.

'Huh?' he said.

'Don't go near him!' I didn't mean to yell, but I couldn't help it.

'Near who?' said Dad.

I looked behind him. The woodland was silent and dark. There was no sunlight. There were no flies. There was no horseman.

'Who was that?' I gabbled. 'What did he want? Why was he dressed like that?'

'Who was who?' said Dad. He still looked dazed; not quite with it, and I had a strong desire to shake him.

'The rider. Over there in the trees!'

Dad looked vaguely into the middle distance and, a little unsteadily, took out his cigarettes. He lit one and stood smoking it.

'You saw him. I know you did.'

He had started to shake. He sucked at the cigarette

the way a man who was drowning would gasp for air.

'Dad?'

He looked straight through me, and I saw something dreadful in his eyes. Something cold and distant and heartless that I had never seen there before. Then he shook himself, as if he was cold, and said brightly, 'Weren't you going home?'

I was speechless.

'I'll be along in an hour or two when I finish up here. You could peel some spuds if you have time.'

He didn't wait for me to reply, but turned and walked rapidly back to the building, flicking his finished cigarette into the gravel at the corner. I stood, rudderless, staring after him. From a branch nearby a magpie cackled. It made me jump. I swung round, stared into the trees, expecting to see the horseman again. The woods were calm and innocent. And dark. It made me realize something that I ought to have noticed at the time. The sky had been overcast all morning with a cover of pale cloud. There had been no breaks in it at all: it wasn't that kind of cloud. So whatever had made the white horse and rider shine as they stood beneath the trees, it hadn't been the sun.

3

It was early afternoon when I got home. Alex was out and the house had never seemed emptier. I wished Mum was there. I was proud of my independence, but just then I could have done with a bit of mothering.

Randall followed me as I wandered from room to room, wondering what to do with myself. In the end I gave in and took him for a walk, but I was jittery and he knew it, and neither of us much enjoyed being out. When we got back Dad still wasn't home, so I peeled the potatoes, washed some broccoli and rooted round in the freezer for some burgers to go with them. There was still no sign of Dad. I phoned Alex on his mobile. I wanted to tell him what had happened, but he was clearly in the middle of something that was more fun than talking to me, and he was answering my questions in monosyllables. I asked him if he was coming home that night, even though I already knew he wasn't. I suppose I hoped he'd take the hint and realize I needed him, but he was having way too good a time to pick up on subtleties.

So I put the potatoes on to boil and then phoned Dad at the lab.

'Hi, Laurs,' he said.

'I'm putting on the dinner. Are you coming home?'

'Might be a bit late.' He sounded cheerful. 'I'm

feeling inspired. I think I could be on the verge of a breakthrough.'

'That's good,' I said, without meaning it. 'But I want you to come home. I want to talk to you about what happened today.'

'Something in particular?' he said.

'Of course something in particular! The horseman!'

He went quiet, and stayed quiet for so long that I began to wonder whether the phone had gone dead.

'Dad?'

He sighed deeply. 'You know, I've been thinking about that as well. I hope you haven't been telling anyone about it.'

'I haven't,' I said. 'Why?'

'Well, you don't want to give people the wrong impression.'

That stopped me in my tracks for a moment. I could imagine how it might sound to someone who hadn't seen what we had. 'What should we do then, Dad?'

'Nothing,' he said. 'We should both sleep on it. I think you'll find that you'll see it quite differently in the morning.'

'Are you saying we imagined it?'

He didn't answer my question. 'Don't worry your head about it, Laurs. I'll be back as soon as I've finished what I'm doing.'

* * *

When Dad eventually came home I had already eaten. I waited while he had his dinner and then went in to help him with the clearing up.

'Dad,' I began, 'what we saw today—'

He cut across me impatiently but he kept his voice calm. 'Do you remember when Alex was little and he used to think there was a big goblin hiding in his chest of drawers?'

'Yes, but—'

'Do you remember what you used to do?'

I did remember. I used to go in and help him take all his clothes out of the chest, then put them back in again so he could see there was nothing in there.

'But this is nothing like that, Dad! I'm not a little kid. I haven't had a nightmare.'

'The principle is the same,' he said, with that irritating studied patience. 'We'll have a look tomorrow in the woods, OK?' While I struggled to find an appropriate answer he went on: 'And do you know what I'm going to do now?'

'What?'

'I'm going to make you a huge mug of cocoa. And you're going to have a good night's sleep.'

Effectively silenced, I accepted the cocoa and took it up to bed. But the good night's sleep was less easy to come by. Despite the cocoa I hardly slept at all. Everywhere my mind turned, the white horseman was there, standing quite still, staring straight past me, his eyes fixed on my dad.

When I went into the lab the next day to start working with the babies, I was as jumpy as they were and it wasn't surprising that I didn't make much progress. Dad seemed to have forgotten about his promise to have a look in the woods, but there was no need for it. I peered in as I arrived and again as I left. There was nothing there. But I didn't forget. The little sleep I'd managed to get had done nothing to change my mind about what I had seen.

Usually when you see something remarkable, the image will stay with you for a while, then gradually fade. With the white horseman it was entirely different. The further I got from the place and the event, the more powerful the memory became. It was as though the image had scorched itself into my consciousness the way a bright light bleaches the retina and stays at the front of your vision long after it's gone. More than that, the horseman grew in my memory. When we saw him in the woods he was life-size. Now, in my mind, he grew bigger, dwarfing the woods, the buildings, the city. I was certain that his appearance had a meaning, and a meaning that was particularly relevant to Dad. It was a warning, though of what I had no idea. I was sure that something dreadful was going to happen.

But as the days passed nothing dreadful did happen, and although the image of the rider and the way he made me feel were never far from the surface, I began gradually to lose my anxiety about it. I didn't mention it to Alex because I didn't want to alarm him, and although I was seeing a lot of Dad in the lab, nothing in his attitude suggested that he had changed his mind about talking. On the surface of things we were getting on well and enjoying working together, but beneath the surface was an uncomfortable tension; a huge, prickly no-go area.

I had a strong sense that something in Dad had changed. It was hard for me to put my finger on it, and it's possible that the change was in me and that I was harbouring a grudge because of his refusal to talk about what had happened. But I think it was more than that. Dad behaved pretty much as he always had. He chatted about the same things, made the same kind of jokes, put the same effort into meeting our needs and being a good father. But something was missing. His spirit was damaged, or in retreat somewhere deep within himself. It was almost as though he was acting being our dad.

I went in to the lab for an hour or two after school every day. Handling the squirrels turned out to be a lot easier than I had expected. I found a good website called www.yourgerbilandyou.org, which told me all I needed to know and a lot more besides. The trick was to let them come to me and not the other way round. I worked on one group of six squirrels at a time. I would open the wire door in the top of the cage, put my hand in and just leave it there. In a surprisingly short space of time, the squirrels would come over to investigate. Provided I kept perfectly still while they sniffed around my hand, they would soon start testing it with their tiny paws, and then start climbing on to it. I learned one important lesson very early on and I was very lucky that I didn't lose one of the squirrels in the process. In every group there were bold ones and timid ones, and it was the boldest of the bold ones that caught me off guard. The very first time she stepped on to my hand she realized that the arm extending above it was an escape route and ran straight up it. In retrospect it was pretty obvious, but I hadn't had the sense to think of it and the gerbil website had neglected to mention the danger. Luckily, as soon as she found herself outside the cage she lost her nerve and hesitated, and in that split second I was able to block her ascent with my free hand. Again luckily, she dropped straight back down inside the cage instead of on top of it. If she had escaped into the room we might never have succeeded in catching her. After that I always wrapped a thick scarf around my arm when I put my hand into one of the cages and the fabric effectively blocked the escape hatch when the squirrels, as they invariably did, climbed upwards.

When they were quite happy standing on my hand and running up and down my arm, the next step was for me to gently start moving. At first the babies would scatter to the corners of the cage, but gradually they got used to it, and then I would bring up my thumb and touch the tops of their heads and their backs. When they were comfortable with that, which didn't take as long as you'd expect, I would start closing my hand over them. To begin with I didn't grip them at all, just let them slide away through the tunnel of my fingers. Slowly but surely I would tighten my hold, letting them get accustomed to the pressure but still leaving them in control. And that was it, really. By the time they were actually picked up for the first time they had come to see my hand as part of their furniture and they were hardly bothered at all. They always wriggled a bit, but they never tried to bite me no matter how firmly I needed to hold on.

The whole process took roughly ten days from beginning to end, depending on the animals themselves and their particular degree of courage. Some adapted much more quickly than that and some more slowly. There were times when it got boring and I half wished I hadn't volunteered to do it, but at the beginning of my second week I was very glad that I had. Dad, after many failed attempts, finally got through to Mr Davenport and told him that he couldn't manage without an assistant. He told me that it had been a 'slightly delicate' situation and that Davenport had put up strong objections, but when Dad told him that I was already going in there on a regular basis he acquiesced and agreed that if I kept a time sheet he would pay me eight pounds for every hour I worked as Dad's assistant. I couldn't believe it. I calculated that I had already earned over a hundred pounds the previous week, which was more money than I'd ever had in my hand at any one time. Things I hadn't even bothered to dream about suddenly became possibilities.

'Don't even think about it,' said Dad. 'You have to put at least half of it into your savings.'

He wanted Mr Davenport to let me have my own card, and fingerprint access. It was vital, he insisted, because I would often be arriving when he was in the inner lab, and it would be far too complicated if he had to come out through the decontamination chamber every time I needed to come in. Davenport resisted. Dad insisted. Eventually Dad won, and was given the codes to enter my fingerprint details on the entry mechanism.

The one thing that Dad hadn't taken into account when I volunteered to help him was what Alex was going to do while we were both at work. Alex said that he was perfectly capable of taking care of himself and didn't mind being left on his own at home, but Dad wouldn't hear of that. So Alex suggested that he could go round to Javed's house every day. Dad said the odd day would be OK, but not every day. Dad wanted him to come along with me to the lab and entertain himself in the woods, but Alex said they didn't make boys the way they used to, unfortunately, and he had no intention of taking up bird-watching or building tree houses. He would only come with us if Javed could come too. They could hang out together; maybe clear out one of the old sheds and put down some practice mats for their aikido. Dad had to consider it. He said Mr Davenport wouldn't like it, but Alex said that since Mr Davenport never showed his face around the place there was no reason he should ever find out.

'Javed won't tell,' said Alex. 'If you get him to swear on it he won't breathe a word. You could trust him with your life.'

'I'm sure I could, but I've no intention of it,' said Dad. But he did, after thinking long and hard, decide to trust him with the secret of the lab and of what he was doing there. It surprised me in one way, but in another it didn't. There was something about Javed that inspired trust.

I don't know why Dad made that decision. Perhaps it was just laziness; the easiest way to get round the problem of what to do with Alex. But sometimes I wonder if it wasn't more significant than that; a sort of unconscious foresight. As though he knew what was coming and needed to have the possibility of a way out. Giving me access to the lab was one of the vital components. Letting Javed in on the secret of its existence was the other. Both those things were to be vital keys to everything that happened on that winter day, when Javed and Alex and I finally realized what it was all about, and took Dad's fate into our own hands.

Not that Javed broke his promise. He swore he would never tell anyone about Dad's work and he didn't. But if it hadn't been for him, things would have turned out very differently.

4

For a week or two at the end of June, Dad was at a bit of a loose end. He had done as much work as he could on researching the genome information. What he needed now was a virus that he could start investigating. He had taken samples of blood from all the squirrels and he found some antibodies, which he kept for future reference, but he hadn't found a single live virus. The babies were all bursting with health.

Mr Davenport had assured him he would find one. The only question was when. While he waited, Dad surfed the Internet and read through all the journals he got on subscription, keeping abreast of the latest developments in the field. When he was burned out with that he came and helped me with the squirrels. 'Civilizing' them, he called it. They needed to get used to his smell and his way of touching them, so the time wasn't wasted. He was as cool and distant as he could be when we were working together, but I could tell that the little ones were getting under his skin. I caught him smiling sometimes as they scurried up his arm, and laughing when they tried to burrow down between his fingers with their tiny paws.

'Maybe we should start a squirrel farm instead,' I said to him once. 'Or a little zoo, or one of those farms where town children go to get bitten by donkeys.'

He laughed, but nothing would make him change direction now. He said I shouldn't give the squirrels names because it would make me too attached to them. They were experimental subjects, he said, not pets, and the only identification we needed was written on their little yellow ear tags. But I gave them all names anyway, partly because it was something to do with my mind while I was sitting there with my hand in the cage. All the red squirrels had names beginning with R and all the grey ones had names beginning with G. There were twenty-four greys and twelve reds, equal numbers of males and females, and I had fun thinking up the names. Some of the babies were quite distinctive, like Rosie, who had a golden streak along her back, and Greg, who had a bit of a squint. But most of them were pretty much impossible to tell apart, so the names, initially, were pretty meaningless really. But I did begin to think of them as pets. It was impossible not to.

They were so, so cute and beautiful and funny. Every last one of them had a different character, and that was why, as time went by, more of the names began to stick.

Each of the small cages had quick learners and slow learners. Smart squirrels and thick squirrels, I called them, though looking back on it I'm not at all sure I hadn't got that inside out. As each one got well and truly domesticated they got rewarded by being moved out of the little transport cages and into the huge, walk-in cages that lined one long wall of the room. Whatever I might have felt about Mr Davenport's project I couldn't fault the preparations he had made for the animals. They had to be healthy or the experiment wouldn't work, so their accommodation was the best that could be built. The room was ventilated by narrow grilles high up on the walls beneath the ceiling so the air was constantly fresh. The big cages allowed the squirrels as much exercise as they liked, and each had a choice of warm nest boxes at different levels. Once they moved into those bigger spaces there was a high probability that they would become wilder again, or 'uncivilized', so I made myself indispensable at the lab by coming in regularly to make sure I could still catch them all.

There were six of the big cages, and eventually there would be six squirrels in each one, divided by colour and sex. The first of them moved into their new homes about a week after I started working there, but three weeks later there were still a few 'thick' ones stuck in the transport cages. One of them was a male grey, that I called Gooch. He used to tease me. I swear he did. When I put my hand into the cage he would come along and climb straight on to it. He would let me stroke his head; he loved being stroked; but the minute I tried to close my hand around him he would make a dramatic dash to the corner of the cage, sending shavings and sunflower husks flying. But he wouldn't stay there cowering, as he would have done if he was really scared. Instead he would come bouncing straight back and hop up on to my open hand again. I guess he wasn't so thick, after all.

Anyway, they're all gone now. I don't like to think about which ones ended up where. In my mind's eye I see them all racing away through the branches, drinking the cold, sweet air that only old trees can make.

5

Dad needn't have had any worries about Javed tipping off the animal rights activists. He was probably the last person in the world who would have done that.

I realized that on the first day he came into the lab. It was a Friday evening after school, and one of the first really sunny days of the summer. I showed him around the complex and ended up giving him and Alex a lesson in rodent handling. Alex was keen and was soon up to his elbow in curious squirrels. Javed hung back, reluctant. Eventually I persuaded him to put his arm into one of the cages, but the instant the first baby touched his hand he snatched it violently away and slammed the wire door closed.

'No way,' he said, almost running over to the sink to wash his hands. 'I don't like them. They are too much like rats.'

He wasn't keen on animals of any description. He was getting used to Randall, but to begin with he had been very nervous of him and even now, if Randall ran to greet him too enthusiastically he would instinctively throw up his hands and back away. When he was bowling during our cricket matches he would keep a rag in his back pocket for wiping the drool off the ball. He always brought several of them, so that as soon as one got too damp he could change it for a fresh one. I thought it was neurotic behaviour, but after the episode with the squirrels he explained it to me and I understood why.

We were taking a lunch break out on the narrow strip of rough grass between the yard and the woodland. I sat facing the trees. I wasn't afraid of being attacked by the white horseman but I couldn't bear the idea that he might be there behind me, watching from the shadows. As long as I could see I was fine.

'I don't know how you can stand picking them up,' said Javed. 'They even smell like rats.'

'What have you got against rats?' I asked him.

'Not just rats,' he said. 'It's different here. You don't have to worry about rabies. But we were always taught to keep our distance from small animals.'

'So you never had any pets?'

'No. My mother hates them. There was a dog at our place in Sunderabad once but it wasn't really a pet. We didn't play with it or take it for walks. It was just there, outside in the servants' yard. It's gone now. I don't know what happened to it. Some people in the city have pet dogs and cats but we don't.'

'You had servants?'

'They are still there, looking after the house,' he said. 'That's the way things are in Shasakstan.'

'You must be stinking rich,' said Alex. 'How come you never told me?'

'You never asked,' said Javed.

Alex and I were quiet for a while, absorbing that, then Alex said: 'Did you ever know anyone who got rabies?'

'No,' said Javed. 'It isn't all that common. But we heard about cases of it in the area now and then. Sometimes there were scares and all the dogs in the street would be locked up for a while, but I never knew anyone who got it. My mother did, though. When she was young, in her village. There was a woman who died from it. No one knew how she got it because she never told anyone that she'd been bitten. She might have been afraid of the injections they give you, or she might have been too poor to pay for them. By the time anyone knew she was ill it was too late to save her. My mother says she can still hear her screams, when she was dying. It has haunted her all her life.'

We were all silent for a while after that, imagining the horror of it. Dad came wandering by, a cup of coffee in one hand and a cigarette in the other, taking the gentle stroll around the yards that constituted his daily exercise. He ought to have been sixteen stone, the way he carried on, but he was one of those people who just never put on weight. When he was out of earshot I lay down on my elbow in the warm grass. Sunlight filtering into the deep green shadows beneath the trees caught the wings of flying insects. Tiny particles of life.

'I don't understand why viruses exist,' said Alex. 'I

mean, that rabies virus. It's incredible when you think about it. The way it spreads itself. What it does to its victims.'

'Its hosts,' I said pedantically.

'Whatever,' he said. 'But it spreads by making its host bite the next one. How does it make them do that? How did it learn to do that?'

Neither of us could answer. He went on: 'I mean, everything has a purpose, doesn't it? Even bacteria can be useful, eating up dead things, making things decay so they don't litter up the planet. But what use is a virus?'

'I don't think everything is useful,' said Javed. 'What use is a mosquito? Or a snake?'

'Useful to who, anyway?' I said. 'You sound like you think there's some grand design or something. Like God worked everything out to suit us.'

'I didn't mean that,' said Alex. 'I'm just amazed that something so tiny, something that can't feel or think, can be so sophisticated. How did it figure out how to make people bite each other?'

'It's more than that, isn't it?' said Javed. 'Any creature that gets rabies becomes terrified of water as well. The other name for it is hydrophobia.'

'I know,' said Alex. 'It's mind-boggling when you think about it. I just can't figure out why something like that has come into existence. What's the point of it?'

'What's the point of anything?' said Javed. 'What's the point of those flies in the trees? What's the point of us?'

'Every kind of life is the same, isn't it?' I said. 'It's main aim is just to reproduce itself.'

Alex seemed quietly shocked by that, and I wasn't entirely comfortable myself with what I was saying. But I went on anyway, thinking aloud. 'It's the basis of everything, isn't it? Even plants. They grow, they flower, they produce seeds and they die. They have developed fantastic ways of inviting insects to help them spread their seeds but it doesn't mean they sat down and thought about how to do it. They just evolved like that. Survival of the fittest. It's the same with everything. Insects, animals, people. Why should viruses be any different?'

'Do you really believe that?' Alex asked. 'That our only reason for being on the planet is to reproduce ourselves and then die?'

I shrugged. 'Have you got any better ideas?'

'There are loads of purposes,' said Alex.

'Like?'

'Like helping other people, or like what Dad's doing: helping other species. And then there's . . . there's . . .'

'What?' I said. 'Cricket? Aikido?'

I felt mean, as though I was engaging in a kind of mental bullying. But Javed was thinking about it and found the words he was looking for at last.

'I suppose helping people isn't really a purpose for being on the planet. Even if you believe in God it's just a way of getting heavenly brownie points. It's more like a kind of social behaviour.'

'Do you believe in God?' I asked him.

'My father says people's religious beliefs should be absolutely private. He says any kind of organized religion just leads to fundamentalism. I think he's right.'

'So does that mean you're not going to tell us what you believe?'

'What does it matter?' said Javed.

'Dead on,' said Alex. 'And since we're all only here to replicate ourselves, I think I'd better go out and start looking for women.'

I laughed. 'You're not old enough yet,' I said.

'Want to bet?' said Alex, raising his eyebrows suggestively.

But Javed wasn't entering into the spirit of it. He was expanding his philosophy, there and then, to fit with the new ideas we were examining 'It's the same as the aikido, isn't it?' he said. 'Our mistake is to think about things too much. It doesn't do us any good. It's like batting. You just have to wait and see what the bowler does. We just have to wait and see what life throws at us and then play it as well as we can.'

'Beautifully put,' I said, lying flat on my back, the sun in my face. 'So let's just lie here and wait.'

But I couldn't relax the way I wanted to. As I lay there on the grass I realized that I didn't trust life's bowler as I had done before. I couldn't see the ball in his hand. I was afraid that when that next ball came down the pitch at me I wouldn't have the faintest idea how to play it.

6

I had been worried that my cynicism might trouble the boys, but I was the one who lay awake half the night fretting about viruses. I couldn't get my head around them at all. From what Dad had told us I knew that they were little more than microscopic strands of DNA which replicated themselves by hijacking the cells of their hosts. Anything that had cells could be attacked by viruses. Even plants got them.

And computers. People spent endless time creating them, just for the badness of it; just because they could. Did that mean that someone – some great hacker in the sky or in the fiery depths – had created human viruses? Just for badness? Just because they could? I didn't believe that for a moment, but I was in awe of the sheer ingenuity of a thing that had no brain; no thought process at all, and yet could send people and animals mad so they had to bite any living creature they encountered. I thought about malaria as well, which got the mosquito to do the work of carrying it, and the plague, which rats could spread around an entire city within days. It gave me the creeps, thinking about those things. The white horseman was big and strong in my mind, still casting a huge influence over everything I thought about. And the fact that Dad was working on the manipulation of viruses was worrying.

I didn't know how, but I was fairly certain that the two were related in some way.

It felt as though I'd only been asleep for five minutes when I was woken by the phone ringing. I looked at my watch. It was six a.m. I was about to get up and answer it when I heard Dad's footsteps and then his voice reacting with rising excitement to whoever was on the line. When he hung up he came straight to my room. Alex, woken by the phone, was behind him.

'I have to go to Wales,' he said. 'They've come across a squirrel that they think has a virus and I need to go up and get some blood from it.'

'What's the rush?' I said. 'It's only six o'clock.'

'Mr Davenport phoned from America,' he said. 'Apparently they found the squirrel yesterday but they couldn't get hold of him until now. The thing's on death's door and I need to get there before it dies, and the virus with it.'

'Can we come?' I said.

'I'm not going,' said Alex. 'It's Saturday, remember? Javed's crowd have got a match.'

'And I need you to hold the fort here, Laurie,' Dad said. 'In any case it would be deadly boring. I'm just going straight there and straight back. I should be home some time in the afternoon. If I'm not you'll have to go to the lab and feed the squirrels.'

* * *

I managed to get back to sleep and didn't wake up till after ten. I had a long shower and a long breakfast, then pottered around my room, listening to music and pretending I was tidying up. I was just beginning to think about going over to the lab when I heard Dad come in.

I met him in the kitchen and put the kettle on. He swept straight past me, keeping as great a distance between us as was possible in the kitchen. I wondered if I was contaminated, but it was himself he was worried about.

'Don't touch,' he said. 'Could have squirrel sneeze particulates on me.'

He ran straight upstairs for a shower, and when he came back down his face was bright red from scrubbing and he had changed his clothes. I put a cup of tea in front of him but he ignored it.

'Have to get this flask straight to the lab,' he said.

'I'll come with you.'

'Good. We'll go on the bikes,' he said. 'Just in case. I was as careful as I could be, but there's the slightest chance I carried some of the virus with me into the car. If our squirrels caught it, it could ruin the whole experiment.'

There was a small steel flask in the kitchen with a temperature dial on the side. I watched Dad as he put on a pair of disposable plastic gloves and meticulously wiped the outside with special disinfectant from a brown glass bottle. Then he put it in a backpack and we went out together to the shed.

His bike was covered in cobwebs and the tyres were flat. Mum's was there, though, in good working order, so he took that and together we cycled to the lab. Dad pedalled like a maniac – I found it hard to believe that he was so fit considering how little exercise he took, but it didn't seem to take anything out of him. He was in a race against time to get the virus alive and well to the lab and into a culture before it died on him. If there was a virus, he said. There was no guarantee that there was. The squirrel had been very sick and had a high temperature but it might have been caused by any number of things.

We parked the bikes and I used my card to open the door in the hayshed. Dad went straight through the cage room and into the 'bug-lock', which is what he called the decontamination chamber between the cage room and the virus lab. I changed into my work clothes, then said hello to the squirrels. They were delighted to see me and clung to the bars of their cages, looking for food and attention.

Whatever Dad was doing took ages. I fed the squirrels and cleaned out all the cages, then handled the slowcoaches until we were all thoroughly bored by each other. I was ready to go home then, but I was keen to know how Dad was getting on and decided to hang on for a while. I turned on the TV but there was nothing interesting on and I turned it off again. The lab buildings were ominously silent and, despite the space and the ventilation, felt airless. I could only imagine what processes my father was going through behind the airtight walls, what alchemical techniques he was using to isolate that tiny string of DNA. I tried not to think about the potential for disaster that lay in what he was doing. I trusted him absolutely, as a scientist and as a father, but no amount of rationalizing could get rid of the sense of unease.

I made a cup of tea and drank it and was just deciding to go home and make a start on the dinner when Dad appeared, stumbling barefoot through the bug-lock door, still in the process of putting on his shirt.

'We've got one!' he said, pushing a button into the wrong buttonhole so that his shirt hung skew-whiff down his front. He wasn't quite punching the air with his fist but he wasn't far off it. 'I'm sorry I was so long but I had to get a few samples set up in a culture. They're breeding away happily now.'

'Well done, Dad,' I said, trying to muster an enthusiasm that I wasn't really feeling.

'Give me a mug of your finest tap water!' he said, reaching for his cigarettes and heading towards the kitchen door. I filled a cup and handed it to him, and he held it up like a toast. 'To my new outside office!'

'Is it that definite?' I said. 'Are you sure you can do it now?'

'Not remotely,' he said, laughing. 'But there's nothing like a bit of optimism, eh?'

He knocked back the water, dribbling a bit down his wonky shirt front. 'Let's go home,' he said. 'I'm exhausted.'

He put on his shoes and stuffed his socks into his pocket. It took longer for me to change my clothes, and he went on ahead of me to get Mum's bike. As I came out of the building I saw him at the side of the first yard, staring into the trees. Even at that distance I sensed that there was something unnatural about the way he was standing.

'Dad?'

He didn't answer. He didn't even look at me. I had seen that look on his face before, and I broke into a cold sweat. I ran to join him. It wasn't until I reached his side that I was able to see what it was that had transfixed him.

The white rider had returned. And this time he wasn't alone.

7

There were two of them, standing side by side. The second horse was the brightest chestnut I've ever seen, its coat shot through with sparks of copper and gold. Its rider was dressed in rusty red, and in his hand he carried a huge sword. Blood was dripping from its tip. The sight scared me witless, but it didn't occur to me to run. Both of us, Dad and I, stood motionless.

They were in exactly the same spot where we'd seen the first one on his own a few weeks before; about twenty-five metres from us, underneath the trees. This time the sun was shining strongly and breaking through between the branches, but it seemed to me, as it had the last time, that they were illuminated by some other, more brilliant source of light.

Both the riders were staring straight at Dad and he, as before, was staring back, totally mesmerized. I don't know where it came from, but I had a sudden strong impulse to remember this; to observe more carefully than I had before. Scared as I was, I managed to keep part of my mind detached, and I looked more closely and saw much more than I had the first time. What I saw was that the white rider was like something out of ancient Rome. His robe was like a toga, and his legs were bare. The gleaming white cape that covered his head and streamed over his horse's hindquarters was held in place at his throat by a huge gold pin. On his head was a crown of bright silver. In his hand he held a bow, and strapped to his calf was a full quiver of arrows.

His horse, as before, stood four square, motionless and calm. The other horse, in complete contrast, was lightly built; skinny and rangy. Despite the fiery glints that bounced off its red coat it looked under-nourished and unhealthy. Even so, it was bursting with nervous energy. It snatched at the bit and danced on the spot continuously. Its rider was lean and, although he hardly moved, I sensed in him the same restless energy. The sword he carried was crude, made of bronze or tarnished steel, but if the blood was anything to go by it was an effective weapon. It should have had me legging it out of there, but it's hard to explain the effect the riders had. I was afraid, but it wasn't an immediate fear for my own safety. I knew, don't ask me how, that the men weren't going to use their weapons on us. The fear they produced was much more subtle. It cut into the deepest parts of my mind; into my soul, perhaps. It overwhelmed me with a suffocating sense of doom. It was so bad that it hurt.

'Dad.' I took his arm. 'Come away.'

He didn't move. I hardly dared look at his face. I tugged at him; tried to turn him towards me. 'Dad!'

He looked absurd, with his shirt front crooked and his face blank and dreamy. It might have been funny, another time. Now it was just terrifying. I shook him frantically, and dragged him round to face me. 'Wake up!'

He looked at me vacantly, as though he had no idea who I was, then turned back to the riders.

I hauled at his arm and tried a different tactic.

'Leave us alone!' I yelled at the riders. I found myself pulling my mobile out of my pocket and waving it at them. 'Get out of here before I call the police!'

They threw the trees at us. That was what it seemed like, anyway, as a sudden, violent wind sprang out of nowhere and bent them all towards us. It tore leaves off them and hurled them in our faces. We put up our arms to protect our eyes, and the leaves hit our hands with so much force that they stung. Then the wind dropped as suddenly as it had arisen, leaving the wood-land quiet and still.

And empty.

Dad took a few faltering steps forward, then changed his mind. His knees were trembling and making his trouser legs shake.

Mine were too.

8

The first time, Dad had sent me home, and later he had fobbed me off with goblins and cocoa. This time I wasn't going to let him off the hook so easily. We were travelling home together so he couldn't get away from me, and there was no way for him to hide how rattled he was. It was a long time before he stopped shaking, and to compensate he cycled at a crawl, leaning forwards and peering at the road as though we were passing through heavy fog.

'What's happening, Dad?' I said. 'Who were they?'

'Mm?' he said, squinting at the clear road.

'You can't pretend you didn't see them. They made you go all funny, Dad.'

'All funny,' he said absently, as though I was an irritating toddler showing him a new toy. He was cycling erratically. He kept trying to drop behind me, but I wasn't having any of it. Whenever the road was clear I rode alongside him.

'You have to talk to me,' I said, with an anger I didn't even realize I was feeling. 'This is scaring me half to death!'

He dragged his eyes from the road for a moment, to look me in the face. In that brief instant I saw that he was afraid too. Terrified. He turned back to the road. 'This project . . .' he said vaguely.

'What about the project?'

But the moment was gone. His guard came up. I saw it, along with the straightening of his back and the raising of his head.

'It's going extremely well,' he said, much, much too cheerfully.

He began to cycle faster, trying to get ahead of me now, instead of dropping behind me. This time I let him go, not because I was allowing him to close the subject but because an idea was beginning to form in my mind and I wanted to think about it. There had to be an explanation for the appearance of the horsemen, and what if it was an entirely rational one? Maybe the animal rights activists had found out about the lab despite all our precautions. What if they had come up with an extremely novel way of trying to scare us off? I could see that it was a bit far-fetched, but it was the best lead I had come up with so far. I was still mulling it over in my mind when we got back to the house.

Alex still wasn't back from the match. Dad bustled around the kitchen being over-cheerful. I left him to it, content now to bide my time and do some more thinking about my new idea. Over dinner Dad made small-talk and I played along. When we were finished he went into the sitting room and I heard the TV go on. I didn't hurry; I stayed in the kitchen and cleared up, giving him time to get settled and let his guard down. But when I went in to join him he wasn't there. I went along to the study and opened the door. He was reading a book. He put it down on his lap where I couldn't see it.

'Just looking something up,' he said. 'I'll be out in five minutes.'

I went back to the kitchen and made coffee. Properly, with the plunger jug and hot milk. I took it through into the sitting room.

'Dad?'

I could hear him moving around upstairs.

'I'm going to bed,' he called back.

'Bed? But it's only eight o'clock.'

'I know. I'm just exhausted. All that driving and everything.'

I went halfway up the stairs. 'I made coffee. I want to talk to you. I've had an idea.'

He came to the top of the stairs. In a sickly-sweet, understanding voice he said, 'Can't wait to hear it, sweetheart. In the morning, though. I'm just too tired now.'

I was furious, and didn't answer.

'Sunday tomorrow,' he said cheerfully. 'Let's all lie in. Egg and bacon for breakfast?'

I drank all the coffee and went into the sitting room, buzzing with caffeine and adrenaline. I stared at the TV screen and saw nothing. Or at least, nothing that was on it. I saw the horsemen. Whether my eyes were opened or closed, I could see them.

Alex came in, with Javed in tow, at about ten o'clock. They were in a subdued mood and both of them slumped down in front of the telly with me.

'What's this?' said Alex.

I hadn't the slightest idea what I was watching. 'Oh, it's just . . . something,' I said.

'We lost the match, thanks for asking,' said Alex.

'Oh, did you? Who were you playing?'

'Warwickshire. I was lbw for seven,' said Javed.

'It was a bad decision,' said Alex. 'Everybody said so.'

'No, bad decision or not, I should have had my bat there and not my pad. I wasn't seeing the ball.'

'Well, don't get depressed about it,' I said. 'You're not the only one who had a bad day.'

'Why?' said Alex. 'Did Dad not find a virus?'

I had almost forgotten about that. 'He did, actually,' I said. 'Listen, you two. Have either of you been talking to anyone?'

'What about?'

'About the squirrels, duh. The project.'

'No, duh. We haven't. We're not allowed to, remember?'

'Can't Javed speak for himself?'

'I haven't told anyone,' said Javed. 'I'll swear on anything you like.'

102

'Why?' said Alex. 'Has something happened?'

I debated briefly with myself about whether or not I should tell them. But Dad had let me down and I badly needed to talk to someone about it.

'Yeah,' I said. 'Something has happened.'

We trooped through into the kitchen and Javed, who couldn't bear the tea that Alex made, put on the kettle and stood guard over it. I knew I could trust the boys. I asked them not to tell anyone, but I didn't have to swear them to secrecy or anything dramatic like that. I just poured it all out, about seeing the riders, first one and then two. I described them as well as I could. They listened quietly, and Javed managed to make a fine pot of tea without clattering anything and disturbing the mood. I could tell they were a bit suspicious to begin with, wondering whether I was pulling their legs or telling a long shaggy dog story, but when I explained my new theory, about the animal rights activists, they seemed much more inclined to believe me.

'Maybe it was a hologram,' said Alex, stirring sugar into his tea.

'Why would someone make a hologram of two riders?' I asked.

'I don't think holograms really exist like that, do they?' said Javed.

'They do in *Star Wars*,' said Alex, who was keen on science fiction.

'There's no way you can go into a shop and buy something that beams two horses into the middle of a wood,' said Javed.

'I wouldn't be so sure,' said Alex. 'They can do anything these days.'

'Maybe,' I said. 'But why would they choose riders?'

'True,' said Alex. 'Not the right style for the animal rights people if you ask me. Bit on the subtle side.'

We all agreed with that, and ruled out activists, for the time being at least.

'So what else could it be?'

'Something from another dimension?' said Alex.

I could hear the radio faintly from Dad's bedroom. He often went to sleep with it on, though I was willing to bet he wasn't sleeping now, no matter how tired he was. But I was glad he wasn't down here with us. We could never have had this kind of conversation if he was.

'I don't think so,' I said. 'They were more like something from another time. Out of the past.'

'There's an idea,' said Javed. 'Maybe there's a special place there.'

'A portal,' said Alex. 'A time portal.'

'Maybe they don't have anything to do with the squirrels,' said Javed. 'Maybe they just slipped through a time portal because it's there.'

'And it might have always been there,' said Alex excitedly. 'Since ancient times. That's why someone built that dirty big wall around the place.'

'Hmm,' I said. 'The only thing wrong with that is the way they were looking at Dad. They weren't interested in me at all. They were definitely there on account of him.'

'But they didn't say anything?'

'No. But I did.' I had a sudden vision of Dad, his shirt front crumpled and lopsided, gazing like a zombie at the riders, and me, my voice high-pitched and whiny, waving my mobile and threatening the apparitions with the police. All the tension of the day found release through that absurd image, and I began to laugh hysterically. It was a long time before I could pull myself together enough to tell them what was so funny. Then I remembered the violent wind that had ripped the leaves off the trees, and I told them about that as well.

'You know what we should do?' said Javed.

'What?'

'We should just go there. Tomorrow. Search the place and see what we can find.'

'Good thinking,' said Alex. 'Then if there's any kind of wiring we'll find it.'

'If it hasn't already been taken away,' I said.

'There's bound to be some kind of evidence, though, if we look carefully enough,' said Javed. 'Broken twigs, bits of wire left around.'

'And we can check out the wall,' said Alex. 'See if there's any way a horse could get in there.'

I wasn't so keen. The memory and the fear were still too fresh. 'You weren't there,' I said. 'You've no idea how scary it was.'

'You can be a victim in life or you can be a warrior,' said Javed.

Alex was a bit more sympathetic. 'We'll get Dad to come if you like,' he said.

My spirits shrivelled. 'Actually,' I said pathetically, 'Dad's a bit weird about it all.'

'Weird?' said Alex. 'What way weird?'

It felt almost impossible to explain, without making me look like an idiot. 'He doesn't want to admit he saw them.' But as I said it, I realized the importance of going. If we found evidence, which I was sure we would, then we could confront him with it. All three of us. Make him talk.

I decided to be a warrior. My spirit was returning. 'Better without him,' I said.

9

I did manage to go to sleep once or twice that night, but never for long. The two riders were in every part of my mind. If I dropped off I woke almost immediately, the horsemen vivid behind my eyes. Once the white rider was bowling at me with a huge, fiery ball, and the red one was keeping wicket behind me, standing right up to the stumps, breathing down my neck. The ball was going to be a bouncer, I knew. It was aimed right at my elbow. Another time the two of them were walking across the sky and I was in a hot-air balloon with Dad. I was trying to blow us away from them, but he was blowing smoke in the other direction, back towards them. He was winning. Every time I woke I would try to push the horsemen out of my mind; to vanish them the way they had vanished themselves. I couldn't, though. They haunted me tirelessly from one edge of the night to the other.

And pretty much every time I woke up I heard Dad's radio, tuned to the BBC World Service, talking to him in his room. He had a sleep setting on it, which meant that it turned itself off automatically after half an hour. The fact that it was on all night meant that he was turning it on again; probably tossing and turning like me. The cheerful face meant nothing then. He was as alarmed by what had happened today as I was. I just wished that he would admit it.

At about three a.m. I heard him turn off his radio, then get up and pad along the corridor to the bathroom and back. Soon afterwards the radio came on again. I turned over and tried to sleep. It was no use. Then I remembered something Mum had once told me: that if you're angry with someone and it's interfering with your peace of mind, the best thing to do is write them a letter. You don't have to send it. In fact in most cases it's better if you don't. But writing it down can help you set your mind at rest. I thought about it for a while and eventually, driven demented by the persistent images, I got out of bed and found a notebook and pen.

Getting it down on paper definitely helped. I made two columns on a clean page, and as I wrote I remembered some things I hadn't thought of before.

WHITE	RED
Appeared first alone.	Appeared later with the white rider. Has not appeared alone.
Wears a crown made of silver.	Has a beard.

Wears white clothes and a long flowing cape.	Wears shabby clothes. Rusty red colour. Bloodstained?
Carries a bow and has arrows.	Carries a crude sword with blood dripping from it.
Horse is well fed and strong. Has a very smart saddle and bridle.	Horse is thin and wiry. Has no saddle and the bridle is made of rope.
Horse is very calm. The reins are loose.	Horse is restless and excitable. One of the reins is broken.
Rider has an arrogant expression.	Rider looks humiliated and angry.

It didn't look much when I'd finished and I wished I could remember more. I read it over a couple of times to see whether anything leaped out at me, but that was about all I could remember. It hadn't helped much. I went back to bed but I still couldn't sleep. I missed Mum dreadfully and wished I could talk to her. And suddenly I remembered that I could.

Dad had put the old computer back in his study, and Alex and I used it for our email. I booted it up. I checked my email then set about composing a message to Mum. I wrote several versions, a few serious ones about what I had seen and the effect it had had on Dad, and then a light-hearted one with the story of the horseman added as a kind of afterthought. But when I read them through they all sounded as if I was going off the rails. I had no doubts at all about what I had seen, but when I saw it in writing it looked crazy. It was making things worse, not better. I deleted the emails and decided to leave it until Mum next came home.

As I was getting up to go back to bed I noticed an unusual book beside the keyboard, half hidden by a couple of printouts. It had a white leather cover that I didn't remember seeing in the house before. Dad was an atheist, and Mum called herself an agnostic, so I couldn't imagine why either of them would have had a copy of the Holy Bible.

Back in bed, still sleepless, I went over what I'd seen, over and over and over. I thought about what I had agreed to do with the boys in the morning but I couldn't remember how I had felt when I decided to be a warrior. I could only remember the fear.

By six a.m. I was so exhausted that I couldn't think straight. I knew that if I didn't get up and occupy myself I was going to go nuts. As I went along to the bathroom I could hear Dad snoring, finally asleep. I envied him, but the fact that he was sleeping sowed the seed of an idea in my head. I was going to have to go through with it; this search I had committed myself to. And if I had to do it, I wanted to get it over with as soon as I could. Why not now?

I didn't fancy my chances with the boys, though. When I went into Alex's room the two of them were in deep sleep. Alex was on the top bunk. I tried him first.

'Alex!'

'Huh.'

'Wake up. I want to go to the lab. I want to search for the riders.'

''Kay,' he said, and turned over to face the wall.

I had better luck with Javed. He opened his eyes as soon as I shook him.

'What time is it?' he said.

'About six. Will you come with me to the lab? To check out the wall and stuff?'

'Why so early?'

'I can't sleep,' I said.

Javed sat up and scratched his close-cut hair. It sounded like someone using a scrubbing brush. He looked dazed but he was definitely awake.

'I'm going to put the kettle on,' I said. 'Can you get Alex up?'

Javed yawned extravagantly and swung his legs over the edge of the bunk. 'I'll try.'

* * *

Half an hour later we were on our bikes and pedalling towards an adventure that I was still in two minds about. It had been Alex's idea to bring Randall with us, and I found his presence reassuring, even though he was a soft-natured creature and would be absolutely useless if we found ourselves in trouble. Mum had trained him to go with her on the bike and he was a hundred per cent road-wise. He ran along beside the back wheel of the last bike and squashed himself in to the verge whenever a car came along. There were very few out at that time on a Sunday, though, and we flew along the quiet roads to the lab.

We parked our bikes in the Dutch barn and walked round to the place where Dad and I had been standing when we saw the riders. There were a few green leaves scattered around, but not as many as I had remembered blowing off the trees the previous day. I hung back behind the boys, surprised by how fearful I still was. I pointed into the trees.

'About there,' I said. 'Under that big beech.'

'Can you see them now?' asked Alex.

'Duuhh!' I said. 'If I could see them you could see them as well! These are horses we're talking about. As in horse-sized horses!'

'All right,' said Alex. 'Just testing.'

'I don't need to be tested, OK?' I was a bit annoyed by what I thought he was suggesting. 'I'm not doolally yet. I saw what I saw!'

We stayed where we were, waiting for that bit of bad air to clear. Randall was sitting at the edge of the trees, wondering whether we were ever going to make up our minds and do something.

'Seek, Randall!' I said.

He bounded up and hared around the place, nose to the ground. After a few moments of that he looked towards me quizzically. I knew what he was saying. 'Seek what?'

The ground beneath the trees was green with wild garlic and bluebell leaves.

'There's bound to be some sign of them in there,' said Javed, moving forward hesitantly. 'They'll have trampled all the plants and stuff.'

Alex and I followed. I was surprised to find that the light under the trees was stronger than it looked from outside. We searched the whole area, treading carefully so that we wouldn't confuse ourselves with our own footprints. Randall sniffed out a trail and tore off along it, his nose to the ground. We watched, hopeful for a moment, but whatever he was trailing appeared to have spent the previous night rambling around aimlessly and circling trees. Before long Randall got disheartened and gave up. So did we. There was no sign of anything: not one broken leaf, not one hoofprint in the powdery brown leaf mould. We craned our necks to see up into the trees all around. Javed gave Alex a leg-up into the beech and he climbed right to the top.

There was nothing unusual there now and no sign that there ever had been.

I was relieved and disappointed at the same time. 'They were definitely there,' I said. 'I swear it.'

'We believe you,' said Javed.

'Do you?'

'I do, anyway,' he said. Alex said nothing. I knew he needed evidence.

We went back to the gates and began walking round inside the boundary wall. Within minutes we were lost, isolated from the world by the wall on one side and the thick woodland on the other. We weren't actually lost; we could always find our way back the way we had come, but we had no sense of where we were in relation to the road, the fields, the buildings. Woods can do that to you. You can walk for five minutes into them and spend an hour trying to find your way out.

The enclosure had a longer boundary than any of us had expected. There were times when we frightened ourselves, convinced that we had entered some kind of dark other world populated by wild riders and who knew what else. Snakes and lions at the very least. Once a passing aeroplane reassured us, and another time Alex helped me to look over the wall, and I could see, among other things, the familiar shape of Worcester Cathedral. And eventually, inevitably, we did get to the end, or rather the beginning; back to the gates again.

114

The wall was completely intact the whole way round. It was never less than two and a half metres high and there were places where the land dipped down and the wall was even higher. There was no way a horse could get in there. Not without a crane or a helicopter.

We walked back to the bikes.

'They were definitely there,' I said hopelessly.

'No one said they weren't,' said Alex. We were all a bit tired and despondent, and I could see why he would be annoyed, after getting out of bed for nothing.

'I know what you're thinking, though.'

'No you don't,' said Javed. 'No one knows what anyone else is thinking.'

I stopped at the edge of the yard and looked into the trees one last time. The day was warming up and the flies were coming out to saunter around in the sunbeams again.

'You know what was the weirdest thing about it?' I said.

'What?' said Alex, less than enthusiastically.

'The reason they were so frightening,' I said. 'It wasn't because they were going to hurt us. I don't think either of us thought that. The scary thing was the hold they had over Dad. He seemed to be completely in their power.'

'But what would they want with Dad?' said Alex.

'I don't know.'

'They didn't say anything, though?' said Javed.

115

I shook my head. 'No, they didn't.' I was struggling now, trying to put something into words that I hadn't really thought through yet. But as I said it I knew it was true, and that it was a breakthrough of some kind. 'The message wasn't something they said to us. The message was them being there. They were the message.'

10

It was ten o'clock by the time we got home. Dad had been out to the all-night garage and the kitchen was full of carrier bags, all half-unpacked. There was a fabulous smell of frying, and Alex and I homed in on the cooker. Dad had two pans on the go, one full of bacon and the other of sausages. Two boxes of eggs stood on the counter-top, their lids open.

'Where've you been?' said Dad.

'Looking for holograms,' I said. 'We didn't find anything, though.'

Dad glanced at me in alarm, and then at Alex and Javed. 'Looking for what?' he said.

'The riders,' I said. 'At the lab.'

'Oh, that,' said Dad, as though he hadn't lain awake all night thinking about it but had recalled it with difficulty from some far-distant recess of his memory. 'Yes, I've been thinking about that.'

'And?' I said.

'I think it was an optical illusion,' he said. 'A trick of the sunlight in the woods.'

'A what?!' I said, completely aghast.

'These things happen all the time,' he said. 'Do you know how many Americans believe they've been abducted by aliens? I mean, really believe that they have?'

'Dad, this was nothing like that and you know it. We saw those riders yesterday as clearly as I'm seeing you now.'

'I know I thought I saw something,' he said. 'But now I'm not so sure.'

I sat down at the table, too stunned to argue with him any more. What he was doing was terrible. Not only was he making me doubt myself but he was making the boys doubt me as well. Javed was looking over at me, and I detected that he knew what I was feeling and sympathized. But Alex was watching Dad dishing out the bacon.

'Only three plates,' he said. 'Javed doesn't eat bacon.'

'Really?' said Dad.

'Or sausages,' said Alex. 'You know that very well.'

'Sorry about that,' said Dad to Javed. 'I forgot you were a vegetarian.'

'Actually I'm not a vegetarian,' said Javed.

'And you can't fry his eggs in the bacon fat,' said Alex.

'It doesn't matter,' said Javed, embarrassed. 'Honestly.'

'I'll scramble them then,' said Dad, reaching for a saucepan. 'I really am sorry, Javed. I ought to have remembered you were a Muslim.'

Alex and Javed exchanged significant looks and Alex shook his head in bewilderment.

'Actually it's not a religious thing,' said Javed. 'I just never acquired the habit.'

He had been through this before and Dad knew the story as well as the rest of us. Javed's dad was a consultant psychiatrist and his mother was an architect turned artist. Like us, they didn't follow any particular religious guidelines. Javed didn't like fry-ups because he found them greasy and unpalatable. Dad was clearly rattled or he would have remembered.

I watched him closely. It seemed to me to be clearer than ever that he was putting on an act, going through the motions of being Dad. I looked at Alex and Javed. Neither of them could see it, I was sure of that. It made my stomach contract with fear. I'd had a fantastic appetite when I came in but Dad's attitude had ruined it. I picked at my eggs and left the rashers and sausages, which gradually became welded to the plate by their own waxy fat. If Dad noticed my subdued mood he did nothing to try and lift it. He chatted, mostly to Alex, about the drive to Wales and the sick squirrel and the virus he hoped was thriving in its culture back at the lab. He tried to include Javed by talking about yesterday's match, but if there were sides at the table that morning, Javed was on mine. I don't know why. I'm not sure that he had any more conviction than Alex did about the existence of the riders in the wood, but he certainly had more empathy with me.

I dropped my leftovers down Randall's hungry

throat, and I was heading towards my room when the phone rang in the hall. I answered it.

'Hi, Laurs,' said Mum. 'Just the person I wanted to talk to.'

The sound of her voice cheered me up immediately. 'How are things, Mum?'

'Great. We're all ready to go on Thursday.'

With all that was going on I'd almost forgotten that the one-day international series was due to start that week. 'Brilliant,' I said. 'We can't wait.'

'Are you all OK?'

'Fine. And you?

'Good, but I haven't got long,' she said. 'I just got a terrible shock. I've forgotten all about the Family Row.'

'It doesn't matter, Mum,' I said. 'We can leave it out for this year.'

'No way!' she said. 'It's a sacred rite! The trouble is that there's only one weekend I can be sure to get away. It's between the third and fourth tests, the weekend of the twentieth of August.'

'That's ages away,' I said. 'What's the panic?' I wanted to tell her about everything: the riders, Dad's behaviour, my hurt feelings. But there was no way to broach the subject. This wasn't that kind of phone call.

'There's no panic,' she said, 'but there's no way in the world that I'm going to be able to organize my team while I'm on the road. Can you do that?'

'Sure. No bother.'

'That means it'll be your team this year. You'll be the captain.'

'No way, Mum!'

But she didn't even stay around to argue. 'Have to run. Love to everyone and I'll talk to you all soon.'

My mood had lifted and I suddenly felt hungry. I wished I hadn't given all my sausages to Randall. I went back into the kitchen and searched around for leftovers.

'That was Mum. She wants to have the Family Row on the twentieth of August.'

'Yess!' said Alex. 'I thought we wouldn't be having one this year.'

'Well, we are,' I said. 'And she's appointed me captain of her team.'

'You're joking,' said Alex.

'I'm not. And I bags Javed.'

'Oh, no!' Alex screamed, but he was laughing as well. He and I never played on the same side, that was one of the rules. We usually tossed a coin to see who would play on which team. So it meant that if I had Javed, Alex would be playing against him.

'All right with you, Javed?' I said.

'Why not?' he said.

'Right,' said Alex, with the air of someone girding his loins. 'Who else are we going to get, Dad?'

But Dad clearly wasn't in loin-girding mood. 'I

121

could have done without this,' he said. 'I'm going to be up to my eyes in the lab.'

'Let Alex do it,' said Javed. 'Let him be your captain.'

'Now there's an idea,' said Dad. 'I always knew you weren't just a pretty face!'

11

Dad gave me a day off work. He said he had to go in anyway and he would feed and water the squirrels. Alex and I made the first batch of phone calls, rounding up our teams. Then the boys decided to practise some aikido and began to rearrange the furniture in the sitting room. I helped them gather rugs from all over the house to lay on top of the carpet and cushion their falls.

From the kitchen I could hear their scuffles, their gasps, the light thuds of their rapid feet on the rugs and the heavier thud when one of them was brought to the floor. They were spending a lot of time at aikido lately. Javed blamed his poor batting performances on his state of mind, and both of them had taken to reading philosophy to help them with their attitudes. When they took their first aikido exam back around Easter time there had been great excitement and Dad had given them the money to go into town and buy their yellow belts. They had decided, though, after long discussions, not to wear them but to stick to their old white belts instead. Showing badges of rank, Alex told me, was against their philosophy. They pursued their art as a means towards improving themselves and not to impress anyone else. Alex had quotes from the *Tao Te Ching* on his wall; things like 'In his every movement a man of great virtue follows the way and the way only', and 'In action it is timelessness that matters', and, my favourite, 'It is because he does not contend that no one in the empire is in a position to contend with him.'

I made myself a cup of tea and took it into the sitting room. The boys paid me no attention, so I curled up on the sofa and watched. They neither encouraged nor discouraged spectators. If their minds were properly oriented, they said, the presence or absence of other people would make no difference to them. If they were put off by people watching it meant that desires or anxieties were intruding, and these were the most difficult opponents; not the person they were sparring with. They did not practise aikido to impress anyone.

They did impress me, though. There was a beautiful discipline about their actions. They were both shooting up like nettles on a dung heap and coming into their adolescent strength, but they had none of the awkwardness of other boys their age. The aikido kept them both as supple and graceful as dancers. In their loose white suits they looked like monks, or strange, ghostly soldiers. They floated, circling around each other silently, watching each other with expressionless faces. Then, when one of them sensed an opening, they would strike with sudden speed and power. Nine times out of ten, the other would block or resist the move with equivalent skill.

Aikido is not about punching power. It's about using the opponent's weight and strength against him. It requires an understanding of how the human body works. If someone aims a blow at you, first you avoid it and then, following through, you catch him off balance and use it to your own advantage. If you can get hold of an arm or leg there are subtle ways to turn or twist the limb which can, if done right, bring your attacker to the ground and completely immobilize him. Someone with good aikido skills can subdue an opponent twice their size and weight.

I think if I'd been forced to choose between them I would have just about given Alex the edge. It wasn't that he was faster, but he seemed able to wait that fraction longer before he reacted. He looked dozy sometimes, his eyelids drooping halfway down over his eyes. But there was a fierce glint beneath them, and when he did react to a move of Javed's, it was with explosive speed. On the whole, though, they were well matched, and the most striking thing of all was their mutual respect. They bowed to each other before and after every round, and when they left the rugs at the end of the practice they resumed their everyday relationship exactly where they had left off. Their quiet, undemanding affection for each other was a model of human friendship.

And more and more that friendship had come to include me. By that time Javed was playing regular matches for the county, and Alex had managed to get himself picked for the second eleven. If either of them were playing a match they invited me, although I rarely went, because of my responsibilities at the lab. We did go mooching around town a couple of times though, shopping for clothes and having a coffee, but what I remember most clearly about those times was the conversations we had. We talked for hours, the three of us, about all kinds of things. Sometimes I think it was because I was lonely that year and had no friends of my own, and that I muscled in on the boys' friendship. And sometimes I believe it was more than that. I believe that our extraordinary fate was already written on our palms or stamped across our brows. If we hadn't had such trust in each other, things might have turned out very differently.

I never understood how they decided when an aikido practice was over. They never said 'Shall we call it a day?' or 'I'm done in.' They would just look each other in the eye, bow deeply to one another and vacate the practice space. On that day, when they had reached that moment, Alex trotted off upstairs to get changed but Javed flopped down on to the sofa beside me.

'Do you ever analyse your dreams?' he said.

'Why would I want to do that?' I asked.

'Just wondered. My mother does it all the time. She tried to get me to do it a couple of times but I could never take it seriously enough. She gave up on me.' He paused, and picked Randall hair off his white trousers. 'I just thought it might be an idea to try and analyse what you saw.'

'But the horsemen weren't a dream,' I said.

'They might have been a vision, though. They must have been, when you think about it, since there's no trace of them.'

I thought about what he was saying and I couldn't deny it. The riders had been a vision. Dad and I had seen a vision. Like people saw moving statues and the Virgin Mary crying and stuff. Did that make it more significant or less?

'I often get inspiration while I'm doing aikido,' Javed went on. 'My mind goes into a kind of meditation. And it came to me, just then. Why not analyse your vision as if it were a dream?'

'How do you do that?'

'Well, you kind of ask questions about things. The symbolism and stuff. You can even talk to the characters if you want to.'

'Can you show me?'

'I can try,' he said. 'It's just a matter of talking about it and seeing what comes up.'

We went up to my room and I got out the notebook where I had written my lists the night before. Javed glanced over it. 'You know, we should call Alex as well.' He sensed my hesitation and went on: 'Three heads are better than two.'

* * *

We went through my lists, one line at a time. We were lying on the grass at the back of the house. Alex had made sandwiches.

'So the white horseman appeared alone first,' said Javed. 'You've put that at the top so does that mean it's the most important thing?'

'I don't think so,' I said. 'I was just trying to be logical about writing things down.'

'It's important though,' said Javed. 'It means that he came first.'

'Well, he did. He was the first one I saw. What's the significance of that?'

'I don't know,' said Javed. 'But this is how you do it. You go through everything and you ask questions about it, even if it doesn't seem relevant. It might be, later.'

'OK,' I said. 'So the white horseman comes first.'

'Who is he?' said Alex.

'I don't know.'

'He wears a crown, though. That must mean something. Is he a king?'

'No,' I said, without thinking about it. 'Or at least, I suppose he might be.'

'He must be if he's wearing a crown.'

'I suppose so. But he didn't look like a king. The crown wasn't exactly like that. It was more like . . . I don't know. It was kind of silver leaves intertwined.

He looked more like a Roman emperor or something.'

'An emperor, then,' said Javed. 'Does that work better?'

'Definitely,' I said.

'OK. So what about the other guy? What about him?'

'He was much rougher,' I said. 'The white rider looked really wealthy but the red one was dirt poor.'

'Would he have worked for him, maybe?' said Alex.

With a sudden flash of inspiration it became clear to me. 'He's a rebel. He's angry, his horse is thin and nervous. The emperor is ruling his land and he's rebelling.'

'A freedom fighter,' said Javed.

'So were they fighting each other?' said Alex.

I shook my head. 'No. But it still fits. It's like they're showing us two sides of the same coin or something.'

The boys seemed to accept this analysis, but the sense of satisfaction it brought me was short-lived.

'And so what?' I said. 'Even if that's what it means, so what? What does that have to do with Dad and the squirrel project?'

Nobody could answer that, and that was the end of it, our analysis session. I don't know whether it had got us anywhere or not, but that night I dreamed about the white horseman. He was enormous; straddling the world. I could see the curve of the horizon under the horse's belly and the blue glint of the oceans. There were flies around him, like there had been in the woods, but when one of them flew close to me I saw it wasn't a fly at all, but a war plane. They all were. There were thousands of them, clouding the air; the show of force of a huge, dominant power. As for the red horseman, I couldn't see him at all. But I knew he was there, waiting in the wings, nurturing his own hidden forces of destruction.

12

It was hard for me to concentrate at school over the following days. I couldn't find any enthusiasm, even for my favourite subjects, and I'm sure some of the teachers noticed that I was quieter than usual. No one said anything, though, and I did my best to keep up, even when my mind was miles away.

On Thursday I took my old transistor radio into school. I had a much smaller one but it didn't get Long Wave, so it was no good for listening to the cricket on Radio Four. It was harder to hide, but it fitted into my school bag and I was able to sneak it out and into a quiet corner of the yard during our morning break.

Alex and I, along with one or two other cricket fans, were listening to the first of the one-day internationals. That was how we became the first ones in the school to hear about what had happened that morning in Birmingham. The commentators kept referring to the morning's 'events' and promising to keep listeners informed of any developments. We turned over to the FM channel and learned that four bombs had gone off in the centre of the city.

I went to the staff room and told the teachers there, and they turned on the TV and got the latest news. There was nothing new about terrorist attacks in England those days. There had been several in London the previous month. But these were the first in Birmingham, and Birmingham, to us, was almost local. When break was over the teachers returned to the classrooms and explained what was going on. Any students who had close relatives in Birmingham were given permission to use the school phones. We were all allowed to have our mobiles on. I sent Dad a text. He was in the lab and hadn't heard anything. He rang us both.

After that the day went on pretty much as normal, but the teachers kept us informed whenever they got new information, and the whole school was in a state of nervous tension. It wasn't until the lunch break, when I had a few moments of quiet to myself, that the connection dawned on me. When it did, a horrible hot tide washed through my bones. The horsemen. The emperor and the rebel. That was what they had come to warn me about. The emperor represented the western world – America, Britain, Europe. The red rider represented the rebellion against their power. Only the red rider wasn't a freedom fighter, as Javed had suggested. He was a terrorist.

It frightened me, but it thrilled me as well. I'd seen a vision, a presentiment of the horror that had struck Birmingham. I wondered whether I ought to have been able to interpret it better, to warn everyone that it was coming. But as the initial excitement wore off, I began to have doubts. The more I thought about it, the less sense it made. Why me? Why Dad? We hadn't been involved in any way. We couldn't have had any effect on the outcome.

I didn't hear a single thing that was said by my teachers during the remainder of the day. My mind went round and round in circles, teasing at what I knew, trying to make sense of it. Emperors, rebels, terrorists. Somehow I was sure that there was truth in that interpretation of the visions, but why they should have appeared to Dad and me, and what their connection with the squirrel project could be, I couldn't begin to work out.

PART THREE

PART THREE

1

A week or so later our school holidays began. From then on I cut my working days down to three a week. I would have been happy to do more, but I couldn't justify taking money for work that didn't need to be done. The squirrels were nearly all manageable by that time, and an hour or two every second day was enough to keep them placid. Once a week, usually on a Saturday, I cleaned out the cages, which was a time-consuming job, and it was my responsibility to keep the whole of the cage room spotless. It worked out to about eight hours' work a week, which kept me in pretty decent pocket money.

On the first Monday of the holidays I got another phone call from one of the coaches on my cricket team, asking me if I was ready to come back. He was really sweet about it; said I could come and go as I pleased, and take my time, and that I wouldn't be asked to play on the team until I was good and ready. To this day I can't understand why I continued to resist. I knew that the only way I was going to get my nerve back was by going along to the practices and getting my eye in again. Cricket was my passion in life. I wanted to play. But instead I mumbled excuses about having a job, and getting twinges in my elbow, and, to my shame, about Dad needing me at home because Mum was away so much. After I put the phone down I stared at it for about ten minutes, hating myself for my cowardice, half hoping it would ring again so that I could change my mind. It didn't. It wouldn't either. I could change my mind whenever I liked, but no one was going to ask me again.

The Birmingham bombings gradually fell from the first item on the news to further down the programme, then disappeared. But they were never far from my consciousness, and although we didn't see them again that summer, nor were the horsemen. Sometimes I almost succeeded in convincing myself that it hadn't happened; that it had all been a dream; but then I remembered my conversations with Dad, and knew that it hadn't been. I still hadn't grasped their significance and it troubled me.

After the bombings there were endless new programmes on the TV about Shasakstan and the increase of Islamic fundamentalism there. It was believed that Bin Laden was hiding out there, and that it was the new centre for Al-Qaeda's operations. There were training camps in the border regions where people went from Britain and other places to learn how to be a terrorist.

I watched them all, and I read articles in the newspapers that never would have interested me before. It seemed to be almost universally acknowledged that the oil wars in the region had been big mistakes, and had opened up a hornet's nest of trouble for the western countries involved. I talked about it with Javed. He said that the present government of Shasakstan was unpopular with the majority of people there because of its close links with America and it was, according to his mother, only a matter of time before it was overthrown by the fundamentalists, who were rapidly gaining strength. I was as absorbent as a sponge, taking in everything on the subject from whatever source I could find. It was a logical step, after the Birmingham bombings, for Shasakstan to become firmly associated in my mind with the appearance of the red horseman. But I could find no such logical step which would shed any light on the connection between the horsemen and Dad's work. Sometimes it drove me half mad, thinking about it, and many times I resolved to leave it alone and forget about it. But I never could. Not quite.

From the first test at Lord's it was clear that the series was going to be a good one. Alex and Javed and I dug ourselves into the sitting room at the beginning of every match and emerged four or five days later, wading through a knee-high drift of crisp, popcorn and chocolate wrappers. Dad joined us whenever he could, and, owing to the tense, close-fought nature of most of the matches, we agreed to allow him to smoke indoors, and his overflowing ashtrays joined the accumulated rubbish.

I think we all suspected that Australia would eventually win, despite the fact that we had beaten them last time, but we also knew that it wasn't going to happen without a fight. They had a dynamic new team who were absolutely determined to get the Ashes back from England. They won the first match but England, by the skin of their teeth, won the second. It was brilliant cricket, and I loved it that Mum was there, watching in the wings, instrumental in keeping the players fit. I was always on the lookout in case I spotted her, but she only ever appeared once and that was when she was replacing the strapping on a fielder's elbow after he'd made a diving stop. There was a close-up of her face and Alex and I cheered and yelled for Dad, who was out making a cuppa. By the time he came in she was gone and, naturally enough, there was no action replay.

She came home on the Wednesday before the Family Row, and the same evening there very nearly was one. A real row, I mean, not a cricket match. She hadn't expected to get away until the following day so she took Dad and me by surprise. She was there when we got home from the lab, and she had already got the dinner on the go.

Alex was at a cricket club party so there were just the

three of us at dinner, and it was brilliant. Dad was thrilled to see her and was flirting outrageously, and she was enjoying it but determined to fill us in on all the latest cricketing gossip. The third test match had been a nail-biting draw. By this stage half the population was following the series on radio or TV, and I felt privileged to be getting the inside track on all the players and the politics. I was perfectly content, but the best was yet to come. Mum had bought a huge cream cake on her way home, and when she put it on the table she dropped an envelope beside it. I opened it and found four Pavilion End tickets for the final test at The Oval.

I leaped up and threw my arms around her.

'It's not until September, so it'll mean you'll have to take a couple of days off school,' she said. 'Do you think Javed's parents will let him come?'

'They'd better,' I said. 'We'll have to kidnap him if they don't.'

We talked about the details; which of our London friends we would stay with and how we would get from their house to the ground, and then I asked who would look after Randall while we were away.

'I'll be looking after Randall,' said Dad.

Mum's face dropped. 'Don't you want to come?'

'I'd love to, but how can I? Who will take care of the lab?'

'But it's only for a few days,' said Mum. 'Surely you can get someone in to take over?'

Dad shook his head. 'You know the way it is with this job,' he said.

Mum shook hers. 'No,' she said. 'I don't think I do.'

With an effort she turned away from him and gave me her 'everything's fine' kind of smile. But everything wasn't fine. The atmosphere was toxic. The cake was too. Dad tried his best to cut it but it behaved like a trifle and he had to use a spoon to get it on to the plates. My splodge of it tasted like polystyrene with whipped anti-freeze. I ate it dutifully, in a heavy silence, then left them to it.

But I didn't go far. I know you shouldn't eavesdrop, but I wanted to hear in case there was anything Dad hadn't told me about the job that I needed to know. Anything that might give a clue as to why mounted emperors and rebels should turn up on his doorstep and look at him.

'I don't see why you're making such a big deal about it,' he said to Mum. 'It's only a match. What difference does it make whether I come or not?'

'It's not about the match,' said Mum. 'It's about what sort of job it is that doesn't allow you ever to take a holiday.'

'But you knew it was going to be like that.'

'I certainly didn't,' said Mum. 'And I'd be willing to bet you didn't either. Or if you did, you didn't tell me.'

'Well, maybe I wasn't thinking as clearly as I should have been,' he said. 'If I misled you, I'm sorry. I didn't intend to.'

'But it's not just about me, James. No one can keep on working like that without a break. It's unnatural. You'll ruin your health.'

'I won't,' said Dad. 'I'm doing what I love. If I was stuck at home all day I'd be more worried about my health.'

'Are you?' said Mum.

'Am I what?'

'Doing what you love?'

Dad sighed but didn't answer.

'Because there's something very fishy about it all if you ask me. A project that's so secret you can't even get a replacement for a few days.'

'We've been through all that,' said Dad.

'Well, maybe we should go through it all again. Like who is this Mr Davenport and why does he keep changing his mobile number, and why do you have to have this top secret lab like something out of James Bond? Why couldn't you have done this research at the university, like you did with the flatworm?'

'Look, love' – Dad said it without sounding as if he meant it – 'I've been working on this project and taking government money for nearly a year now. Do you want me to turn round and say, "Oh, I'm sorry, I've changed my mind"?'

'Well, how much longer is it going to go on?' said Mum. 'How many more years?'

Dad's voice brightened a bit and became conspiratorial. 'I'm not making any promises but I think I might not be too far off. I've discovered a significant difference in some of the cells in the nervous system. I'm going to start investigating it very soon. I think I know where I'm going. It's just impossible to say exactly how long it's going to take to get there.'

Mum waited.

'If everything went really well it could be a matter of months, or even weeks.'

'And if not?'

Neither of them said anything for a while, and I heard them moving around the kitchen, gathering the plates and loading the dishwasher. Then Mum said, 'And you're not worried about the ethics of it?'

There was a long pause, then Dad said quietly: 'I am, as a matter of fact.'

'Really?' said Mum.

'Yes, really.' His voice was thin, as though he was speaking with a great effort. It was the old Dad, I'm sure, not the actor Dad, coming to the surface for a brief time. 'I think about it every morning when I'm going to work and I think about it every evening when I come home. But the thing is, we haven't got there yet. There's a strong possibility that we never will; that the whole thing will have been a waste of time like the flatworm. But I need to know, you see? I need to pursue it as far as I can. For myself, not for anyone else. For the pure science of it.'

I think he got us both with that one. Mum and me. I said nothing, of course, because they didn't know I was listening. Mum said: 'So you don't really have to decide on the ethics until the last minute? And then only if it works.'

'Exactly,' said Dad. 'I can burn the lot at the end of the day if I decide to.'

That was his get-out clause, I realized later. That was how he justified what he was doing; what he surely must have known he was doing. He believed, deep down, that he wouldn't have to go through with it. But I think he was wrong. I think the horsemen already had him completely in their power.

2

'So who's going to use the fourth ticket then?' Alex asked. It was Friday afternoon and we were putting the final touches to the pitch. Alex had done the outfield with the ride-on mower and had left snazzy parallel lines. It looked brilliant. I had marked out the crease with white chalk powder and checked that the pitch didn't have any particularly nasty bumps or cracks.

'I don't know,' I said.

'Why don't you bring one of your mates?' he said.

'Because I don't have that kind of mate,' I said, and at that time it was true.

'We'll find someone for it,' said Alex, to cover the awkward silence that threatened to follow my admission.

I nodded. We cast a final eye over the pitch and went back inside.

The first cricketers began to arrive an hour or so later. There were friends of Dad's from school and friends of Mum's from various teams she had played in through the years. Dad's sister always came with our three cousins and it was usually the only time we met during the year. They stayed in the house, but everyone else brought tents which we all helped to put up on the lawn and in the orchard. The weekend of the Family

146

Row was total pandemonium. The house was always heaving with people and if you wanted a shower you had to put your name down on a list on the blackboard outside the bathroom. When it was your turn the person before you would come and find you. But apart from that it was brilliant. We got to meet friends and relatives that we only saw once a year, and in the evenings, weather permitting, we had a mega barbecue in the yard.

Because we could never be sure how many would turn up, we invited everyone and worked out the teams when they had all arrived. There was no limit to the number of players on each side, but the fielding side was only allowed to have eleven players on the pitch at any given time. Whoever was off the pitch had to help make tea or soup or sandwiches. Players under ten were given a go with the bat but they weren't allowed to field because it might inhibit some of the stronger batsmen from having a slog. The only cricketer who didn't enjoy himself that weekend was poor Randall. For obvious reasons he wasn't allowed to play, and because there was no way of keeping him in the house with all those people wandering in and out he had to be tied up outside the back door. He got plenty of attention and an enormous quantity of scraps, but the Family Row was not a happy occasion for him.

People who lived locally didn't come until the Saturday morning. That year, for the first time, Javed's family were among them. I had met his parents a few times when one or another of them had collected him from the house, but I had never really got to know either of them and I had never seen his two older sisters at all. They were both at university, one at York and the other at Cambridge, and they rarely came home. They were there under protest, I felt, and spent most of the time nattering in the kitchen. But Manir and Attiya Malik were a different kettle of fish. Attiya had never played cricket in her life and was a total waste of space on the pitch. She couldn't bat or bowl or catch and she couldn't even throw straight. But she was one of the funniest people I've ever encountered and her deadpan commentary on the game more than made up for her lack of ball skills.

She wasn't by any means the only one who couldn't play. The Family Row was, above all, a weekend of fun. If anyone was considered to be taking it too seriously they were punished by being sent to make tea, even if they were the captain. Especially if they were the captain. But there was room for a bit of good cricket as well, and when Javed's father came in to bat for the first time it was immediately apparent to everyone where his son had got his passion for the game. Manir Malik was a fantastic amateur cricketer. He was a quiet, graceful batsman and his spin bowling was so good that he had to modify it for most of the time because he would have run through half the opposing team in a couple of overs. He saved his best bowling for the top players like Mum and her friends. They were up to it, but only just, and there were a couple of ding-dong battles on both days of play.

The tradition in the Family Row was that it should always end up with the scores level. If the teams were poorly balanced they would be reshuffled following the first innings to even them up. There was no limit to the number of innings each side could have. Provided it didn't rain, the match ran until four in the afternoon on Sunday and the last session was always hilarious, with whichever side was winning doing its best to let the other side level the score. That particular weekend the weather was spectacular, and the 'pavilion' – the shed where we kept all the gear – was knee-deep in floppy white hats and bottles of sun screen. The last ten minutes of play was a riot. The scores were level but Dad and Manir were still at the crease and had to stay there until four. They couldn't score any more runs, but in the spirit of the game they had to pretend that they were trying to. I was captain, and it was my job to make sure they didn't get out, so I had put Attiya on to bowl to her husband. Mostly she bowled way off target, but on occasion she sent one down that managed to dribble up towards the stumps. When that happened he would nudge it away, and then he and Dad would start off for a run, then pretend to change their minds and dash back again, even though their stumps were never in any danger. I bowled myself from the other end and teased Dad by sending him full tosses which he had to prevent himself from smashing to the boundary. But when four o'clock came the score was still unchanged and since both teams had achieved the required result we were all triumphant. I think it was the best Family Row we ever had.

Mum stayed on until Tuesday, and so did most of the aunts and uncles, and cousins and some of the friends as well. I didn't get a moment on my own with Mum, and even if I had I'm not sure I would have told her about the riders. It wasn't that I didn't want to bother her. She was my mother, after all, and she had the right as well as the duty to know about anything that was troubling us. But the match had lifted my spirits and I was happy for the first time in weeks. I didn't want to go back to that gloomy place in my mind where the riders were, even if I could find a way of telling it that sounded convincing. I just wanted to forget about it and enjoy the time with Mum.

The match had promoted Javed's parents to the position of family friends, as opposed to merely parents of a family friend. They stayed for the barbecue on both nights and fitted seamlessly into the established gathering. Attiya was particularly popular, entertaining whoever she was talking to with her zany humour. She had a wonderful take on life: she could make anything seem funny, even if it was tragic. I spent a lot of time hovering nearby and wishing I could see things like that. Meanwhile Dad and Manir seemed to have hit it off spectacularly well. When the local players were leaving and we were standing together waving off each car-load, Dad asked me whether we had found a taker for the fourth test match ticket. I said that we hadn't, and he said he knew someone who would love it.

So that was how Javed's dad wound up coming with us to the Oval test, and how another piece of our curious fate fell into place.

3

Javed said his dad nearly fell off the floor when he offered him the ticket. Manir worked in criminal psychiatry and spent his time going around the country doing consultancy work for the courts. He was a bit like Dad in that he never stopped working. He did take holidays, though, once a year, but it was nearly always to go to Shasakstan with the family. He had never spent much time in London and had never attended a test match anywhere in England. He wouldn't have thought of it himself, but when he was presented with the possibility of a ticket he was determined to go, and immediately set about rearranging his schedule. There was one day that he was unable to go because he had a court appearance that couldn't be changed, but luckily it was on the first day of the match, so he wasn't going to miss too much.

Mum was insistent that he stay with the rest of us at her friends' house in Kentish Town, but he wouldn't hear of it. He booked himself into a swanky hotel near The Oval, but he let Javed stay with the rest of us. That way, he said, everybody would be happy.

The boys went up to London on the Wednesday evening before the match. I was to go with them, but we had the first hockey practice of the year that evening after school. I had missed the cricket season, but I was determined to get back into some kind of sport, and I didn't want to miss the practice in case I changed my mind again and backed out. I could have taken a later train but it would have got me into London in the dark, and I preferred to get an early one in the morning and go straight to The Oval. I sent my bag with Alex so that I wouldn't have to take it to the match and lug it around all day.

But I ended up taking a bag anyway. I was just getting dressed when the front doorbell rang. It was only 5.30 in the morning so it was pretty surprising. When I got downstairs Dad gestured towards a new black and purple backpack on the floor beside the door.

'Attiya dropped that in,' he said. 'Javed forgot it yesterday and I said you'd take it for him.'

It weighed a ton. I couldn't imagine what was in it. On the train to Paddington I heaved it on to the overhead ledge, making a mental note to myself not to forget it. These days everyone was ultra-conscious about security, and a left bag could cause endless disruption.

But it wasn't until I got on to the tube that the first, horrendous moment of suspicion crept into my mind. I was sitting opposite a dark-skinned man. He had a rucksack on the floor between his knees, and despite the new security systems on London transport I couldn't help thinking about the spate of suicide bombings that had caused them to be introduced. As though he had read my thoughts, the man leaned down and opened the rucksack and took out a bottle of water. He appeared to be making a point of revealing its contents – a laptop computer, a file of papers, a loose-leaf pad – and I wondered whether this had become a routine with him. He looked nice. It was unfair that he should feel the need to prove his innocence. After all, anyone could be a bomber. Nothing said you had to be dark-skinned or even male. *I* could be a bomber.

I looked at Javed's backpack, and that was when the thought hit me. I had no idea what was in it. What a brilliant way to carry out an attack, to plant a bomb on a nice, middle-class white girl that no one would ever think of searching.

I'm ashamed of the thoughts I had then. It was the horsemen that laid the seed of them, I'm certain of that. I don't believe that I would ever have begun to entertain them if it hadn't been for that ongoing, unsolved mystery of why the riders had appeared that day, so soon before the Birmingham bombings. The trouble was, once they had started, there was nothing I could do to stop them. What was in that backpack? Why was it so heavy? Javed was one of the most organized people I knew. Had he really forgotten to take it with him? Or was there another reason he had asked his mother to give it to me?

It was absurd, I knew it. There was no way Javed would do a thing like that. He was a peaceful, gentle character who would never harm anyone. But I began to think about some of the things he had said. He had been critical of fundamentalism, but he had been very critical of western aggression against Muslim countries as well. He was angry about the occupation of Afghanistan and Iraq, and the recent invasion of Iran. So what? A lot of people were. But then, there were things about Javed that I didn't really know. He didn't eat bacon or sausages and he said it was because he didn't like them. Maybe that wasn't true. Maybe he was secretly a strict Muslim. Maybe that was why he insisted that people's religious beliefs should be a private affair.

Was that why the horsemen had appeared to me? I looked at the bag, and a cold prickle of fear touched my heart. Even then I was ashamed of my thoughts, but I couldn't change them. I wanted to open Javed's bag and see what was in it, but I couldn't do that either, because that would be to give way to the fears I was try-ing to deny. It would be to admit that I suspected him of something unthinkable, and I didn't. I swear I didn't. But I couldn't get rid of the fear. What if Javed had nothing to do with it? What if Attiya or Manir had sent the bag? It wouldn't work. There was a witness. Dad was a witness and they would be caught. And anyway, they were our friends, fine people. They just wouldn't.

I looked around the carriage at the other people in there. Ordinary people making their way around the city, like those others, the victims of the other attacks over the last few years. Their journeys would have been like this. Normal days, just like any other.

The train pulled up at a station. I wanted to get off, leave the backpack behind me or ditch it on the platform – anything to end this dreadful conflict. I waited. It was only a matter of seconds while people got off and others got on, but it seemed to take an hour. At last the train pulled away again. I was still in a cold sweat, but by staying where I was I had faced down my demons. By the time we got to the next stop I had banished those crazy ideas from my mind. I knew there was no bomb in the bag and I had re-established my faith in Javed and his family. But there was no escaping the realization that I had, even for a short time, allowed myself to suspect my friends, and for no other reason than their nationality. No amount of self-recrimination could change the fact that it had happened, and no amount of rationalization could stop that brief and poisonous episode from returning, at a later stage, to sway my mind again.

When I got off the train at The Oval I found Alex and Javed waiting for me outside the station. Javed took the bag and shouldered it. He seemed surprised by the weight of it, and took it off and opened it.

Inside was a box of chocolates, a bottle of expensive whisky and a huge, lethal weapon of a coffee-table book full of spectacular aerial photographs of Shasakstan.

'Presents,' he said. 'For your friends. For putting me up in London.'

It wasn't the best match of the summer, but it was pretty good. The fourth match had been another draw, which meant that there was everything still to play for. Australia needed to win it to take the Ashes. All England needed to keep them was a draw, but we were all hoping that we'd win and take the series cleanly. There were a few breaks in play because of rain, and after the third day it became clear that the most likely outcome was going to be a draw. It became clear, that is, to everyone except the Australians. They played like lions, determined to win the series against all the odds, and it made for fantastic cricket. From the first ball the match engaged me entirely, and for a few wonderful days I forgot about everything except the cricket. I forgot about emperors and rebels and viruses, and about my shameful suspicions about Javed and his family. People who have only seen cricket on the TV sometimes think you wouldn't be able to see much from the edge of the ground because you don't have the benefit of close-in cameras. It's not true. You can see way, way more if you have a good seat. You can see the ball swing in the air or move off the seam. You can see exactly where the batsman hits it and whether or not a chasing fielder is going to stop it before the boundary. And you can see the diving catches as they happen, and not just in action replay.

From the second day onwards, Manir Malik was with us. He was bursting with enthusiasm. He couldn't stop talking about the Family Row and how much he had enjoyed it, and about how he would never again go for a year without coming to see at least one test match. Although he said he was supporting Australia, I think it was just to wind us up. In a more serious moment he said that the only matches where he really cared who won were between Shasakstan and India. Otherwise it was the game that mattered; the strategies and the quality of the players. He applauded good play whenever he saw it, which set a good example to the rest of us, and he filled up the hours when rain stopped play with stories of great matches he had seen, or gossip about some of the great Shasakstani players of the past.

The Australians put up a tremendous fight, and for a while it looked as though they might break through and snatch the series. But England's tail-enders refused to give up their wickets and in the end we held out and kept the match to a draw. The crowd was delighted and, if you didn't know, you might have been forgiven for thinking we had won the series. It was brilliant to be there and a part of that delight. On the train on the way back to Worcester Manir told Alex and me that he owed our family a huge debt of gratitude for bringing cricket back into his life. He told us that he wouldn't forget it and that he'd find a way of showing us his appreciation. We said the best way he could do that was by coming and playing a few overs with us on the odd weekend and he said he certainly would. But we didn't realize that he had something else up his sleeve. Something far more exciting.

It was a couple of weeks later that I heard about it. We had settled back into school. I was in Year 11 and heading into GCSEs so I was having to knuckle down to some hard work. I was in training with the hockey team and beginning to feel less socially isolated. Two days a week I had practice after school and on two other days I worked in the lab with the squirrels. I did a half day there on Saturday as well, so my days were pretty well occupied and I didn't have much time to worry about the horsemen. In any event, time blunts the sharpest edge and, no matter how momentous the visions had been at the time, they were fading in importance with each day that passed. Like an unsolved case file: still open but slowly making its way to the bottom of the pile.

Mum had been home for a couple of weeks after the end of the Ashes series, but she had gone back to work with some of the injured and recovering players in the hope of getting them fit for the winter season. We had caught up with each other properly this time and got used to being a family again. It had given Alex and me strength for the next stretch of time without her, and Dad too, I think. But when Alex and Javed broke their news to me the Sunday after she left, the bottom fell out of my world again.

'We're going to Shasakstan,' Alex said. 'Javed's dad is taking us!'

I was stopped in my tracks, inundated by a torrent of conflicting emotions. 'Who's we?' I said at last, half hoping that the plan didn't involve me. It did, though.

'All of us,' said Alex. 'You, me, Javed. Dad's fixed it with the school already. We'll be away for two weeks altogether. Just before Christmas. We're going to see the one-day international series.'

'Neat,' I said, trying to sound as though I meant it.

'And you know the best thing? We're not going to tell Mum. Promise you won't tell her?'

'I promise.'

'And we're going to surprise her. We'll just walk in one day. Can you see her face?'

I could imagine it and the thought cheered me up a bit. The boys began discussing where we were going to stay and what else we would do when we were there, but I didn't stay to listen. I slipped off quietly to my room and lay on my bed, staring at the ceiling.

I didn't want to go. I was afraid. Since the bombs in

Birmingham and the association I had made between them and the red horseman, I had been interested in Shaskastan, and had read everything I could get my hands on. But nothing I had learned had made the place seem remotely attractive. I knew from what Javed and Manir had told me that there was plenty more to the country than the fundamentalist faction, but the thought of going there just filled me with dread.

'Do you know where your passport is?' said Dad as he was driving me back from the lab after school the next day.

'It's in my desk.'

'Is it up to date?'

'Yes. Why?'

'Because we have to send it off to the Shasakstani embassy. To get your visa.'

I said nothing for a while, and Dad kept glancing at me, questioningly.

'Are you OK?' he said.

I shrugged. 'Do I have to go?'

'No,' he said. 'Of course you don't. But you'll regret it if you don't. It's a fantastic opportunity.'

'I know,' I said. 'I know it is.'

We arrived at the house and got out of the car. Dad usually left me to take my bike off the carrier but this time he came round to help.

'It's perfectly safe, Laurie,' he said, pulling the

161

quick-release strap in the wrong direction and tightening it instead of loosening it. 'I've had a long talk with Manir and he says there's no way he would take Javed, let alone you two, if he thought there was any danger at all. And I wouldn't let you go if I didn't believe him.' When I said nothing he went on: 'Do you think they'd send the cricket team there if it wasn't safe?'

I took the end of the strap from him and released it. 'I suppose not,' I said. 'But what about . . . ?'

'What about what?'

'The horsemen,' I said, broaching a subject that had been taboo since the day we saw them.

Dad huffed noisily. 'You're not still thinking about that nonsense, are you?' He dragged the bike roughly off the carrier and plonked it on the ground. 'Look, you really don't have to go if you don't want to. But Manir had to pull all kinds of strings to get hold of those match tickets. It would be a bit of a let-down for him if you changed your mind.'

I wanted to say that I hadn't changed my mind because I had never been asked whether I wanted to go in the first place, but there seemed no point.

'Imagine your mother's face,' Dad went on, 'when you walk in and surprise her.'

That almost swung it, but not quite. Hot on its heels came the memory of that day on the tube in London and the terror I had felt. Rationalizing it didn't help. Whether it made sense or not, the associations between the horsemen and Shasakstan were too strong.

I took the handlebars from Dad and began wheeling the bike towards the shed. 'I don't want to disappoint Manir,' I said, 'but I'm not going.'

A couple of days after that I got a surprise visit from, of all people, Attiya. She asked Dad if we could use the Internet, and we went off together into the study. She showed me a website devoted to Shasakstani tourism. I had to admit it looked wonderful.

'I'm going to come clean,' said Attiya, 'and admit that I've been sent here. On behalf of Manir and Javed. They want you to go to Shasakstan and they want me to persuade you to go.'

I wasn't surprised. Alex and Javed had been on at me constantly.

'I can perfectly well understand why you wouldn't want to go there,' she said. 'It's a bit of a mixed-up place. It's governed by a military dictatorship and it has a growing fundamentalist problem. I can't deny any of that. It's one of the reasons Manir and I wanted to settle here in England.'

She hit a link and showed me a picture of the president, in military uniform, and then another of a woman in a black veil, which hid her face.

'And then the Americans came along and made it all worse,' she said. 'They started this radical Islamism as a way of getting the Russians out of Afghanistan. Now they can't stop it. They have a huge military base in Shasakstan trying to get it back in its box, but the trouble is it won't lie down again. The extremism just keeps growing.'

'So why should I want to go there?' I said.

'Because you will love it.' She hit a new link on the website and showed me pictures of a modern shopping mall, with young men and women looking pretty much like young men and women in any modern city. No uniforms. No veils. There were links to restaurants and cinemas, computer and mobile phone shops, gifts and crafts and antiques. Worcester might try and advertise itself in just the same way.

'But this is Shasakstan too. They want tourists and they take care of them. You won't be going anywhere near the troubled areas. Do you think I'd let Javed go if I thought there was any chance of danger?'

She changed the page again, and I saw pictures of stunning mountain landscapes, of wonderful old forts and palaces and museums. I couldn't deny that it looked fantastic, but my heart was unmoved.

I shook my head. 'I know you wouldn't. It's not that. It's just . . .' Attiya waited until I was ready to continue. 'It's just that I had a . . . a premonition or something. I just have a bad feeling about the place. It scares me.'

Attiya laid her hand on mine. 'Sometimes we have

to face the things that frighten us,' she said gravely. Then, in that characteristic way of hers, she erupted into laughter. 'And sometimes we have to run away from them as fast as we can. If you feel that it's not right then you definitely shouldn't go.'

After the conversation with Attiya I felt better about my decision to stay at home. I just wished that Alex wouldn't go either.

Dad helped him fill in the visa form and sent it off with his passport to the embassy in London. I held on to a pathetic hope that it would be rejected, or that it might fall down behind a desk in some dark corner of the Shasakstani embassy and not be returned until after the next spring cleaning. But the passport, duly stamped with a visa, turned up in the post only a week or so after we had sent it away. Manir bought the tickets for the flights and Dad, after a long battle of wits, finally succeeded in getting him to take the money for Alex's. The next step was a visit to the doctor to get jabs and prescriptions for malaria tablets. To Alex the trip was a huge adventure on a distant horizon and he just couldn't get there quickly enough. But for me, December seemed much too close for comfort.

Mum had a few weeks at home before the Shasakstan tour. The boys' trip was kept strictly secret from her, because of their determination to surprise her at the first match in Chandralore. She spent loads of time with us, but we didn't do much as a family, all four of us together, because Dad seemed to take Mum's presence as an excuse to spend most of his time at the lab. And when he did come home, that absent quality that I had seen in him since the appearance of the first horsemen seemed more evident to me than ever. I was going to mention it to Mum when the right opportunity came along, and use it as a way to bring up the subject of the horsemen, so when she suggested we go for a cycle together, just the two of us, I agreed willingly.

It was a beautiful day and we were dawdling along, enjoying the autumn colours and stopping now and then to pick blackberries. There was all the time in the world, and I was going over the subject in my mind, thinking of the best way to approach it, when Mum said:

'Do you mind me being away so much, Laurie?'

I was taken by surprise. 'No,' I said, without thinking. 'Why?'

'I just want you to know that you can always talk to me about things. You can send me an email and I can ring you, if you're worried about anything.'

'OK,' I said. The door was open. I was about to mention Dad's behaviour, but she wasn't finished.

'It's just that your dad said he's been a bit worried about you.'

'Did he?' I suddenly saw it coming. He had got to Mum first.

'He said . . . well . . . he said you'd been seeing things.'

I should have confirmed it with her there and then, but I was on the back foot. It was like the time I'd tried to send her an email. It looked crazy then. It would sound even crazier now to try and explain that Dad had seen things too, but wouldn't admit it. His tactics were brilliant. If I hadn't been so angry I might even have admired them. Instead I tried to think on my feet and turn it around.

'I'm fine, Mum. It's Dad I'm worried about. Don't you think he's acting weird these days?'

'Weirder than usual?' she said.

'Yes,' I said. 'Don't you think he's kind of distant or something? Not quite with us?'

Mum burst out laughing. 'What's new?' she said. 'The story of my marriage, in a nutshell.'

While I was trying to think of a better way of explaining it, she went on: 'Don't worry about your dad, sweetheart. He'll snap out of it as soon as he gets where he wants to go. Then he'll be back to his usual self. He's nutty as a fruitcake, your dad. You should know that by now.'

I wanted to follow that up; to say that 'nutty as a fruitcake' didn't come near it. But Mum had a dreamy look of affection on her face and I knew that, just then, she wasn't going to hear any criticism of Dad. Usually I liked it that my parents were so mad about each other, but just then I hated it. I felt as if they had formed an alliance against me, and I was struggling on my own to hold on to the truth.

Maybe I should have told her, even if it did make her think I was cracking up. She might have stayed at home and become involved with what happened. She might even have found a way of stopping it all before it came to crisis point. I doubt it, though. I don't think Mum – or anyone else for that matter – could have foreseen what was going to happen, or imagined what was lurking in the shadows around the lab, waiting for its moment to appear.

Alex's fourteenth birthday was on the twenty-third of October. He made the usual jokes about catching up with me. For most of the year I was two years older than him, but because my birthday wasn't until January there were always a few weeks when I was only one year older.

By a coincidence that was hardly surprising, Alex was given two hakamas that day: one from Mum and Dad and the other from Javed. It was slightly embarrassing, but there was an obvious and very happy outcome when Alex persuaded Javed to keep one of them. They looked to me just like long black skirts but I have to admit that when the boys wore them to practise their aikido they looked brilliant; like a pair of young Samurai warriors. I promised myself that as soon as I could I'd start going to classes. As soon as Dad finished with the squirrel project.

By the time of Alex's birthday Manir had finalized the itinerary for their Shasakstan tour. He had a fabulous programme worked out for them. The first two one-day internationals were in Chandralore, the third in Hamachi and the final two in Sunderabad. Hamachi was hundreds of miles to the south, but there were three free days on either side of that match, so Manir and the boys were going to use the time to have a little tour and see a bit of the country.

I remembered the pictures Attiya had shown me and for the first time I felt envious. I would have loved to take those trips. There was probably still time to change my mind, and I considered it. I didn't, though. I couldn't.

A few days later, along with the team, Mum left.

The tour was to start off with three five-day test matches at different grounds around Shasakstan. We got cable TV so that we could watch bits and pieces of the matches when they coincided with our free time. There was some great cricket. Javed, who joined us at weekends, said that Jamali, the Shasakstani captain, was the most under-rated batsman on the world scene. He said there was no one who played the ball later than Jamali, or with such grace, and I had to admit that his batting was a pleasure to watch. Javed recorded all his innings and studied them later at home, and that autumn Jamali took over from Sachin Tendulkar as his role model. Manir expressed huge relief at this turn of events. Despite his internationalist temperament he had never been quite comfortable with having a son who idolized an Indian cricketer, and he had been trying for years to convert him to Jamali.

Our own temperaments had become a bit more internationalist by then as well. There was a lot of banter between us as we watched the matches, with Javed cheering for Shasakstan and Alex and me supporting England. But Javed said Alex would get lynched if he was caught shouting for England when they were in Shasakstan, so he had better get in practice before they left. It was a joke, but Alex went along with it, and worked hard at learning the names of all the Shasakstani players and the proper way to pronounce them. Which, as Javed observed, was more than most of the English commentators did.

We made our smoking allowance for Dad again, but I don't think he joined us once. He spent every spare moment at the lab. We missed him.

The test series ran right up until the end of November, and then the team had a ten-day break before the one-day series began. For the first week of December Alex was like a cat on a hot tin roof. He had finished his packing before the end of November, and his rucksack sat in the hall outside his room like an

171

eager collie, waiting to be off. He had a money belt with his passport in, and some sterling and a credit card, which Dad had got for him specially for the trip. He left the belt sitting on top of the rucksack, and on two separate occasions I saw him open it and examine the contents.

'Just checking,' he said. He would, I decided, turn out to be one of those people like Mum, who had to check three times that the gas was off and the back door was locked before she left the house. But he would also be one of those people like Mum, and not like Dad, who kept a tight ship and always knew where everything was. I felt very close to him during that last week before he went away, and had to work hard to prevent myself ruining his fun by being too anxious. I realized we had never in our lives been apart from each other for more than a few days at a time. When he went to Shasakstan I would worry about him, but I would also miss him. He knew my email address, but just in case, I wrote it out in clear letters and tucked it carefully away in his money belt.

I said goodbye to him on Thursday morning, the eighth of December. When I came home that evening the rucksack had disappeared from outside his door, and he was gone.

5

I checked my email regularly. The first one from Alex was there when I got up on Saturday morning. They were five hours ahead of us in Shasakstan, so by the time I read the email they would have already been at the first of the one-day matches. But even before they saw any cricket they were having a brilliant time. They were staying with one of Javed's uncles in a huge old colonial house in Chandralore. Alex's spelling went to bits as he raced through his report, telling me about the trees and the amazing birds and insects all around, even in the middle of the city. The uncle was a bigwig in the army, Alex said, but you wouldn't know it. He was really nice and funny, and he was cricket mad as well. He had two daughters a bit older than me who were into the city nightlife and were really disappointed that I hadn't come. I have to admit that I felt a bit of regret as well, when I read it. It sounded exotic, from Alex's descriptions, but also quite normal and safe. My anxieties for him evaporated.

Dad had already gone to the lab by the time I got up, but I didn't go until the late afternoon. That way Dad and I would be leaving together and I could get a lift home. I watched the second half of the one-day international on TV, searching the crowd shots for Alex and the Maliks. I didn't see them, but England won the match, so I was in good form when I set off to work. It was a wintry day with a strong west wind, but cycling soon warmed me up and I got to the lab just before the rain started. Inside the squirrel room it was warm and dry. I changed into my work clothes and set about cleaning out the cages, and it wasn't long before I realized that one of the grey squirrels was missing. I did a quick headcount and discovered that there was a red one missing as well. I inspected the cages carefully but I couldn't see any way they could have got out. Even so I went round the cage room, searching in corners, making my feeding-time call. All the others responded, emerging from whatever nest box or corner they were in and climbing up the nearest wall of their cages. But there were still two missing.

Dad was in the virus room. I called him on the intercom.

'Hi, sweetheart. You ready to go already?'

'No,' I said. 'I've just got here. But there's a couple of squirrels missing.'

'They're in here,' Dad said.

'What are they doing in there?'

'Being dissected, I'm afraid.'

I was too shocked to reply.

'I'm looking for those nerve cells I was telling you about. Now we have to see if the reality fits the theory.'

I still didn't know what to say. I was battling with

emotions. The shock had been replaced by sorrow, and by humiliation as well, because I ought not to have been feeling like this.

'Sweetheart?'

'Oh, yeah, that's fine, Dad,' I managed to say. 'But you should tell me, you know, when you take them. They're my responsibility, after all.'

'Sorry,' he said. 'You're right. Bad practice on my part. It won't happen again.'

I closed the connection and went back to the cage room. I was furious with myself for being such a wimp but I couldn't get rid of the distress I was feeling. Whenever I blinked I visualized the two of them spread-eagled on the dissection board, their innards open to the air. I had done dissections myself at school and I'd never had a problem with them: I had been the scientist's daughter, hard-nosed and strong-stomached, laughing at my squeamish class-mates. But then I hadn't known those frogs and rats. This was different. I had tamed those young squirrels. I had made pets of them so Dad could catch them and kill them.

I wished now that I hadn't given them names. I had to make a point of not checking the ear tags as I cleaned out the cages. If I didn't notice who was there I wouldn't be able to tell who wasn't. But I was much too familiar with them all. No matter how hard I tried not to, I soon knew perfectly well which ones were pinned out on that board.

Dad knew me better than I liked to think. On the way home he was sympathetic and conciliatory, even though I refused to admit that I was upset. I was irritated with him at the best of times, but that evening it was all I could do to restrain myself from biting his head off. The day had been an emotional rollercoaster and all I wanted to do was go home and let it all settle.

We stopped to get a Chinese takeaway; another conciliatory gesture from Dad. We ate it at home, then I checked the email. There was a new one from Alex.

He had been to the match and was full of himself. The cricket had been brilliant, but the best bit had been when they surprised Mum during the lunch break. He said she had just stared at him for ages as if she was seeing things. But then she realized he was really there and the celebrations began. He and Javed got introduced to both teams. Javed got Jamali's autograph. They were both allowed to stay on the England balcony for the rest of the match. Eat your heart out, Laurie. He didn't say it, but I heard it all the same. I was beginning to feel totally spineless for backing out. At that moment I could hardly even remember what it was that I'd been afraid of.

Dad came in and read the email over my shoulder. There was one from Mum as well, telling us the story from her side. It made me feel even worse. Pathetic. The warrior who wasn't.

* * *

On Monday evening as we drove home from the lab I asked Dad if he'd found the nerve cells he was looking for.

'I found nerve cells,' he said. 'Too early to say if they're different in the way I want them to be.'

I nodded and looked out of the window for a while. Then I said, 'Why did you take on this project, Dad? What are you hoping to get out of it?'

He shrugged. 'I don't think I want any more out of it than I'm already getting,' he said.

'Really? Don't you want to win the Nobel Prize or anything?'

He laughed and did his Einstein impression. Most people would have thought it was Hitler, and I was glad he rarely did it in public. 'I can't see it, can you?' he said. 'I don't think I'll ever be famous.'

'You'll get this published, though, won't you? If the experiment works.'

'Lord, no. It's all far too hush-hush. I couldn't publish even if I wanted to. It's written into my contract.'

Since I had eavesdropped on his conversation with Mum that day I had felt less worried about Dad's work. I'd believed what he had said to her then, about being free to pull out if the experiment looked like working. But hearing about the extent of the secrecy gave me goose pimples about it all over again.

'Then what do you want out of it?' I said. 'Is it just money?'

'Money's nice,' he said. 'And the self-esteem, when you do something that hasn't been done before. But it's more than either of those things, at the heart of it. It's the beauty of science. Pure science. If I wasn't getting paid for it I would still do it, just to see if I could.'

'Like Everest,' I said. 'Because it's there.'

'Something like that,' said Dad. 'Or maybe it's the only way an atheist can get close to God.'

Those words reminded me of something. Later that evening I remembered seeing that copy of the Bible in the study. But when I asked Dad about it he only shrugged dismissively.

'It's an interesting sociological document,' he said. 'No home should be without one.'

⚜ 6 ⚜

Most of the one-day internationals happened on days when I had to go to school. I sometimes watched or listened to an hour or two in the early mornings, but I never got to see a whole match from beginning to end. The next email from Alex filled me in on the important details of the second of them, which Shasakstan won. He also told me about the previous day, which he had spent exploring Chandralore with Javed and Manir. They had been to the bazaar in the old part of town, and to some of the old monuments: mosques and forts and ornamental gardens. Alex had fallen in love with the city and the Shasakstani people. He was determined to visit the country again, and for longer next time. When that happened, he promised, he would drag me along with him, whether I liked it or not.

He warned me that this would probably be the last email I would get for a while. They were setting out for Hamachi the next day and were going to do some sightseeing along the way. He was looking forward to it, he said, and felt completely comfortable in Shasakstan, wherever they went. He couldn't wait to head out into the countryside.

Over the next few days I felt increasingly sorry that I hadn't gone with him, because it was around then that

179

Dad's behaviour took a definite turn for the worse. He began to spend longer and longer hours at work. The days were shorter now, but despite the early darkness I would cycle straight to the lab from school, even if it was pouring with rain. I tended to go there as a matter of course now, on the days when I didn't have hockey practice, even though there was hardly anything for me to do any more. The squirrels were all healthy and confident, and giving them feed and water only took a few minutes. But that was where Dad was to be found, so that was where I went. It became our routine.

He was always working in the inner lab those days, and when I arrived each afternoon I would check in with him on the intercom. When I was finished, if he hadn't already come out, I would call him again and let him know. If he was ready he'd give me a lift home, and if he wasn't I would wait around until he was finished. I often got all my homework done in the little kitchen there. But over those days in December I had far more time than I needed, and I often found myself at a loose end. Two or three times I had to plead with Dad to come out and take me home, and after that he embarked upon a new routine, which was to drop me home when I was ready to go, and then return to the lab after dinner.

And even dinner times were shortened. More often than not we would take a detour through town and pick up a takeaway. To begin with it was a treat, but I soon lost my appetite for those stodgy, lukewarm meals. I spent too many evenings on my own, watching rubbish on TV and waiting for Dad to come home. A few times I waited up until after midnight, and eventually went to bed in an empty house. Sometimes I woke when he came in during the early hours of the morning. Other nights I didn't hear him come in at all.

More squirrels vanished from their cages. Despite Dad's promise to tell me when he was taking them, he invariably forgot. I noted down the tag numbers of the missing ones and tried, unsuccessfully, not to remember their names. Some of them broke my heart. I ought to have been consulted about which ones were used first but I didn't press the point. Bad as it was to discover that my favourites were missing, it would have been ten times worse if I'd had to choose which one was next for the chop.

It was clear that Dad was hugely excited about the progress he was making on the project. He was in a state of constant nervous agitation, speedy and jumpy. He smoked non-stop wherever he found himself, and he never sat still for a moment. But whenever I tried to question him about what he was doing he was evasive and refused to give me any details. Looking back on it now, I think I know what was happening with him. He was engaged in a terrible battle between his conscience and his pioneering spirit. I think that, whatever he had said to Mum, he now really believed that the experiment was going to work. And I suspect he knew something else as well, something he would never have admitted to anyone, perhaps not even to himself. I think he knew what the appearance of the horsemen had presaged, and what the connection was between them and the project. He can't have guessed, though, exactly how the final part of the story would involve him. If he had, I have no doubt at all that he would have stopped what he was doing then, before it got too late.

I hated the way he was behaving: his driven, single-minded selfishness frightened me. It pervaded everything; the atmosphere at home and the atmosphere in the lab. Even the squirrels seemed to sense that something dreadful was happening, and were uncharacteristically quiet and tense, as though they were watching something that I couldn't see. Every time I came and went from the lab I examined the shadows beneath the trees. I was certain, though I never saw them, that the horsemen too were waiting.

It was a lonely time for me. I missed Alex and wished I'd gone with him. Mum kept in regular contact, which was something, but although I told her Dad was working a lot, I didn't burden her with my loneliness. It wouldn't be long before they were back, after all. And then everything would be all right. That's the thought I hung on to, anyway.

* * *

The last two one-day international matches were to be played on the nineteenth and the twenty-first, in Sunderabad. Mum was due to fly back the following day, which was a Thursday, but Alex and the Maliks were staying until the Friday; just two days before Christmas. Mum sent me an enormous list of all the stuff we had to get in to be ready for Christmas. She wasn't going to have time for everything when she returned, so Dad and I would have to get ahead with the organization. The perishable food would have to wait until the last minute, but we would make life a lot easier on ourselves if we got the presents and most of the other stuff out of the way earlier. So on the Saturday before the Christmas weekend, I tried to persuade Dad to come with me into town to make a start on the list. Knowing the mood he was in, I'd been careful to give him plenty of warning, and I'd reminded him several times that week. But when it came to it he ducked out. He said the work was at a critical stage and he just wanted a few more days. I had come to the end of my tether and we had a big row about it, but he wouldn't back down. The best he would do was to drop me in town with a promise to collect me again in the afternoon. I arrived in the centre in a foul mood, but for a few hours I managed to forget everything and drowned my sorrows in pure, unadulterated consumerism.

On the way home Dad asked me what he should get Mum and Alex for Christmas. I told him he was going to have to free up a small part of his busy mind and work that out for himself.

In the event, he didn't get them anything. He can be forgiven for that, though, in view of what happened next.

7

Attiya Malik always said she did her best work in the early mornings, before the family was awake. That was how she came to be in her studio on the morning of the twenty-second, when the news first came through on the radio. She rang us straight away.

I was woken by the call, and heard Dad galumphing down the stairs. I thought it was probably mad Mr Davenport, who often phoned at unsociable hours, and turned over to go back to sleep. But I could hear the alarmed tone of Dad's voice even though I couldn't hear the words he was saying. It had me on my feet and down in the hall before I could even think about it.

He was just hanging up as I got there.

'What's happened?' I said.

I could hear the fear in my voice. Dad looked bewildered. He shook his head as though he might shake the nightmare out of it. 'That was Attiya. She says there's been a coup in Shasakstan.'

'What does that mean?'

Dad still looked bewildered. For a long moment he stood there, staring at the phone. Then, with a suddenness that made me jump, he turned and raced upstairs. 'Get dressed,' he called back to me. 'We're going out!'

* * *

In the Maliks' sitting room Attiya was sitting in front of the TV, watching the 24-hour news channel.

'I knew it would happen,' she said, turning the volume down. 'I just didn't think it would happen so soon, or so dramatically.'

'What's going to happen to the children?' said Dad.

'That's the problem,' said Attiya. 'They have closed down all communications, according to the news report.' She turned to me. 'Your mother will be all right because they have allowed the cricket team to leave. But it was the last plane out. The airports are all closed.'

'Good God,' said Dad. 'What are we going to do?'

'I think we should go and meet your wife at the airport and then we can all work out what to do next. In the meantime there isn't much we can do.'

We sat in silence for a few moments as Dad and I absorbed the gravity of the situation. One of Javed's sisters phoned, and Attiya chatted to her for a long time. When she came back she turned up the sound on the TV. Everything she had told us was confirmed.

'It's clearly an inside job,' said Attiya.

'How can a coup be an inside job?' said Dad.

'The Islamist faction in the army got too big to be contained any longer,' said Attiya. 'The best way for power to change hands was for them to stage-manage a coup. It's the Shasakstani version of a cabinet reshuffle.'

I listened to her with one ear and the TV with the other. Expert after expert was trundled out to explain who was behind the coup and what it might mean for the state of world politics. But none of them gave us any clue as to what might happen to people who were stranded in Shasakstan, and none of them yet knew the extent of the drama that the new leaders were about to unleash on the world. We didn't hear about that until we were well on our way to Heathrow.

Dad decided to drive because there was no knowing where we might have to go later to try and find out about the boys. On the car radio we heard more about the coup. The new government had made an announcement. They demanded the release of several key Islamist leaders who were in American prison bases throughout the world and called for all foreign troops to be removed from the Middle East. They had banned all but their own military planes from Shasakstani airspace. The US forces based in Shasakstan were to be considered hostages until their demands were met.

Dad laughed when he heard that. 'Why should the Americans take any notice of them?' he said.

'Because they're scared of them,' said Attiya.

'How could they be scared of them? Look what they did to Afghanistan and Iraq. There wouldn't be much left of Shasakstan if they sent in the bombers!'

'But they can't do that,' said Attiya. 'Shasakstan is

not the same as Afghanistan or Iraq. This new president, whoever he is, has his finger on a very dangerous button. Don't forget that Shasakstan has nuclear weapons.'

My blood ran cold. Now I understood. The horsemen, white and red, sent their vicious wind blowing through my soul. Was this the reason they had appeared? To warn of this? To prevent me going, so that I wasn't trapped there now, like Alex and Javed and Manir? Whatever the meaning, it was coming to pass. This, without a shadow of a doubt, was connected with them.

Heathrow was heaving with excited people. There were battalions of journalists and photographers waiting to interview the England team when they got off the plane, though the focus of their interest was not the team's victory in the one-day international series but the new situation in Shasakstan. There were dozens of policemen as well, some of them heavily armed. We were there early and had a long wait, with nowhere to sit or even lean. We got coffee after coffee, but all of us were too anxious to eat.

Eventually the flight arrived. We waited again, more anxiously than ever. It seemed to take for ever before the first passengers emerged. The police formed a cordon to help the cricket team get through the crowd. Cameras flashed and journalists called out, but no one on the team had any comment to make. They looked shocked and disheartened, hardly the mood for home-coming heroes. But, as I learned later, they had only just heard what had happened in Shasakstan. The army tanks had rolled on to the runway as soon as their plane had left the ground, but even though they had been so close to the drama, they were the last to know. If news had reached the pilots on the plane, they hadn't relayed it to the passengers.

There was no sign of Mum, and it was noticeable that no Shasakstani people were emerging into the arrivals area. A few more bewildered-looking travellers wandered out, and then I saw him.

'Alex!'

I dug Dad in the ribs with my elbow, then barged my way through the press of people to meet him at the barrier.

'How did you get here?' I said, hugging him hard. But he just shook his head, and when I pulled back I saw that his eyes were red with tears.

8

While we waited for Mum, Alex told us what had happened.

The previous evening Manir had thrown a post-series party for some of his cricketing friends. One of his cousins worked at the local TV station and he had brought three videos containing the highlights of the entire one-day international series. There were vast quantities of food and drink which everyone enjoyed, but the real business of the evening didn't begin until the videos were put on.

Altogether there was six hours of footage on the videos, so the party looked like going on all night. But at about two thirty in the morning there was a phone call for Manir. It was very brief and when he came back he said it had been a wrong number. But Alex knew him well enough by then to see that he was badly shaken. He did his best to hide it, but the ambiance of the party had changed significantly. Everyone watched the TV for a few more minutes, until some-one suggested that it was very late and maybe they should all go home. In dribs and drabs the company filed out into the avenue, woke their sleeping drivers and started for their homes.

When the last of them was gone Manir told Alex and Javed that he had to go out for a while, and while he was gone they should pack. They had to be ready by the time he got back. He didn't tell them what was going on, and both of them were bewildered and frightened.

When he returned, they set out for the airport. He told the boys he had been out to arrange for some cash, but he wouldn't tell them what was behind the sudden change of plan. 'I thought it would be great fun if we could all travel back on the same flight as the team,' he said, but Alex and Javed didn't buy it. It was clear that something very bad was going on and that there was nothing they could do except trust in Manir's resourcefulness to get them all out of the country.

The airport was almost deserted and the ticket desks were closed. Manir left the boys with the bags and set off through the airport to find someone with a greasable palm and the authority to sell him tickets.

They waited. The London flight was scheduled to leave at ten forty-five and the departures board declared it to be on time. Check-in time was three hours before that, because of the rigorous security routine at the airport. By then it was about six, and it was another hour before Manir came back. He gave Alex a ticket and his passport.

'Javed and I are the first on the waiting list,' he said. 'There are bound to be some free seats. I'm sure we'll get on.'

'I'm not leaving Shasakstan without Javed,' said Alex.

'Of course not,' said Manir. 'I'm sure you won't have to.'

He went off again, and a while later Alex saw him talking to people who were lining up at the check-in desk for their flight. Javed told him that he was trying to get people to sell him their tickets, but no one would. Soon after that the team showed up, and Manir persuaded Alex to go and join Mum. It was time to check in. He didn't want to leave Javed, but Manir made it clear he had no option. He was still optimistic that they would all get on the flight.

Three hours later, after thorough security checks and a lot of waiting around, Alex and Mum boarded the plane. The cabin crew were prowling the aisles and checking seat belts when one last, breathless passenger appeared at the cockpit end of the aisle. It was Javed.

The plane doors closed. Fifteen minutes later it was airborne.

The rest we knew, and filled in for him. Alex nodded thoughtfully. 'Javed's uncles must have known it was going to happen,' he said. 'One of them must have made that phone call to warn us.'

Mum had her wits about her when they got to Heathrow. She and Alex were ushered through like royalty with the cricket team, but Javed was taken aside by the police. Mum asked what they wanted and they told her that they needed to ask Javed a few questions. Mum refused to leave him. After a long argument they agreed that she could be present during the interview, but not Alex. He didn't know how long it would take so he decided to come through and wait for her in the arrivals lounge.

It wasn't just Javed who was being questioned, clearly. It was a long, long time before we saw any people with dark skin emerging, and then there were long intervals between them. We learned later that some Shasakstani nationals had been detained for several days, but Javed, luckily, wasn't one of them. He and Mum arrived about forty minutes later. We were all delighted to see each other, but our celebrations didn't last long. They couldn't. Someone who ought to have been there was missing. Manir was still stranded in Shasakstan, and none of us knew how long it would be before we would see him again.

PART FOUR

1

It was the strangest Christmas ever. Dad, who had been shocked into reality by the fear of losing Alex, took a break from the lab. He went over once a day to look after the squirrels and check his cultures, but came straight home and swung into action, making endless phone calls to the Home Office, the Foreign Office, the Shasakstani embassy and anyone else he could think of who might be in a position to find out what had happened to Manir. Attiya was doing the same thing on her own phone with about as much, or as little, success as Dad. At every step they were stone-walled. No one, it seemed, had any influence whatsoever with this new government.

When he reached the end of the line with that, Dad wandered around the house, tidying in his usual in-effectual way, and asking regularly if Mum wanted him to do anything. But, uncharacteristically, Mum was equally dithery. Occasionally she tried to put her mind to the festive occasion, but with all that was going on in our world and in the wider world beyond, it was hard for her, or for any of us, to get into the spirit of feasting.

It was Attiya who rescued the day. She dropped round with Javed on the morning of Christmas Eve and invited us all to spend the following day at her house.

'I propose we all opt out for the day,' she said. 'Turn off the TV and the radio and leave the religious maniacs to slug it out between them. We'll have a nice, secular feast, just for the hell of it. And the only rule will be that we are not allowed to talk about politics.'

She must have been aware of the shock we all felt at her words. With her husband out of contact and her country at the heart of a new world disorder it seemed almost callous to turn her back on it like that. She laughed at our expressions of disbelief.

'Worry never robbed tomorrow of its sorrows,' she said. 'It only robs today of its strength.'

So we dressed in our everyday, comfortable, secular clothes and went over to the Maliks'. For a non-Christmas. It was a great day. Attiya had laid on a wonderful meal of varied origins, and for the first time in days we put the worries of the world out of our minds and enjoyed ourselves. We played cards and charades and board games instead of watching TV, and Attiya, as always, had us all in stitches. But for all she had said about worry, and for all her clowning and laughing, I glimpsed, from time to time, the sadness in her eyes. There was no doubt that she missed Manir terribly.

At about midnight Mum and Dad began to make 'time to go' sort of noises, and Alex asked if he could stay the night with Javed. Attiya said he could, and that I could as well, if I wanted to. The boys seemed keen, so I agreed. Attiya dropped Mum and Dad home because she was the only adult who hadn't been drinking, and the rest of us went upstairs to Javed's room. I assumed I'd be sleeping in the spare room, but Javed dragged a chair-bed into his room from the landing and made it up for me.

We got into our beds and lay in snug silence for a while. Then Javed said, 'It's after midnight. It's Boxing Day. We can talk about whatever we like now.'

I wasn't sure I wanted to be reminded of all those things I had worked so hard at forgetting, but after a while Alex took the lead.

'So, it looks as if we were right about the horsemen all along,' he said.

'Right about what?' said Javed.

'About what they were telling us,' said Alex.

'Well, what were they telling us?' said Javed.

'You know. What we said. About the empire and the rebellion and everything. That's what happened, isn't it?'

I waited for Javed to respond to that, but he said nothing.

'I think they might have been warning Dad not to let Alex and me go to Shasakstan,' I said. 'After all, if I had gone, who would have had the last ticket home?'

'I wish you had gone,' said Javed. 'I wish I was still there with Dad. I didn't want to leave him.'

'But if I hadn't been there either, then you would

199

both be back here.' Javed didn't respond to that, and Alex went on: 'He'll be OK, Javed. I know he will.'

We had been through this endlessly, Alex and I. We had decided that Javed's uncle, whichever of them tipped Manir off, would have manoeuvred himself into a safe position within the new government, whatever his personal philosophy. He would make sure Manir wasn't harmed.

'I wish I could be so sure,' Javed said. A bright spark of anger flickered in his eyes. It wasn't aimed at us, but it unsettled us all the same.

'So you don't think the horsemen meant anything?' said Alex. 'You don't think they were warning Dad against letting us go to Shasakstan?'

'I don't know what they were doing there,' said Javed. 'I didn't see them.'

I experienced a twinge of anger myself at that. 'You didn't see them so you don't believe I did either. Is that what you're saying?'

Javed softened. 'I didn't mean that. I just meant that I can't get worked up about it. If they had told us how to stop the coup happening it might be different.'

I hated what was happening to us. We'd had such a great day, with everyone entering into the spirit of Attiya's politics ban. But now we had been drawn straight back into the storm at the centre of world affairs and all of us, especially Javed, were still being affected by it. I sensed that he felt the horsemen belonged to a more innocent past, as if they were a game that we had once played or a Famous Five mystery that we had tried to solve together. There was no point now in trying to revive that lost interest. I had to go along with the interpretations we had put on their appearance, but I didn't believe that we had seen the last of them. They were with me constantly those days, standing like a backdrop to the political situation and to all my thoughts connected to it. Still hovering around the woods, watching the project. Still waiting for something. But for what?

✂ 2 ✄

Despite the restrictions imposed by the new government a certain number of eye-witness reports did get out of Shasakstan. There were a few journalists there with satellite phones and for a while at least they were able to send out messages. Other accounts were smuggled out across the borders and sent from neighbouring countries. Most of them were in agreement on the immediate aftermath of the coup. There had been arrests and detentions but very little bloodshed: at least, not yet. But severe new religious laws had been passed which affected the way people lived, and they were being strictly enforced. The general consensus of the reports was that the people were knuckling under and keeping their heads down. What would happen in the longer term was anybody's guess.

Meanwhile the US government was coming under pressure at home and abroad to come up with a peaceful solution. More and more critical voices were heard in the media, expressing the view that the rise of Islamic fundamentalism was a response to the policies of the West in Muslim countries. It was time, almost everyone agreed, for America to take the lead in making some significant changes. Since there was no military option available to it this time, the US administration had no alternative but to adopt the diplomatic route. The White House issued a succession of strong statements asserting that it would never give in to terrorism, but it was well known that negotiations about the release of the prisoners and the withdrawal of US forces from the Middle East were taking place at undisclosed locations. In the meantime the stalemate continued, and the world held its breath and waited to see what would happen.

During the week between Christmas and the New Year Dad took more time off work. He spent no more than an hour or two there each morning, and the rest of the time he was at home with us. I was delighted. The trauma we had lived through had clearly freed his mind from whatever hold the horsemen had on him, and he was himself again. Not acting, not distant and scary. He was my dad again and I capitalized on it. I got him out to the cinema, and for walks and cycles. We had a few centimetres of snow one day, and he joined Alex and me in making a snowman. I laughed at his jokes even if I'd heard them before. Maybe I was the one who was acting now, but it felt great, having him back.

I spent a lot of time with Mum as well, but I still didn't manage to tell her about the horsemen. In one sense, the global one, they were more present than ever. But in another, now that Dad was fully with us again, they seemed less significant. I wasn't needed in the lab those days so I didn't have to pass those creepy woods and imagine what might be lurking in them. I couldn't see any purpose in dragging myself and Mum into that darkness, particularly as there was a chance that we wouldn't have her at home for much longer.

On the first day of the new year she was due to go to a conference in New Zealand called 'Developments in the Treatment and Rehabilitation of Serious Sporting Injuries', but now she was in two minds about going. The conference only lasted three days but she had arranged with some of her colleagues months ago that they would take an extra week or so to have a bit of a holiday while they were there, so she was due to be gone for a fortnight. The flights and the conference had been paid for by the management of the team but, given the situation, they had left it up to Mum to choose whether she would go or not.

She had pretty much decided not to, but by New Year's Eve the situation in Shasakstan hadn't changed. The nuclear holocaust we had all half expected hadn't happened. Shasakstan was still the top item on the news every day, but the researchers were hard pressed to come up with any new angles. It looked like being a long-term stalemate rather than the sudden and total collapse of civilization that some commentators had been predicting. In view of that, there was nothing to be gained by Mum hanging around at home, and although her employers were putting no pressure on her, she felt under an obligation to them. Alex and I were getting on with our lives and Dad was planning to get back to some serious work in the lab the following week. In the end, with our blessings, Mum made the decision to go.

3

I don't know why it was that Mum was never there when the most momentous things happened. For some reason she had no part to play in the drama that had started to unfold and that was soon to reach its climax. And since she had no part to play, there was no need for her to get mixed up in any of it. At least, that was what her fate seemed to have planned for her: to be the one who heard about it all after it had happened, and who had to help pick up the scattered pieces of her family's lives. Perhaps it was her punishment for having been away from us so much. After the fire she gave up her job anyway. She had to, because someone had to look after Dad.

Javed, however, was clearly destined to be involved. Why else would he have been at our house the night Dad got that critical phone call from Mr Davenport? If Mum had been there instead of in New Zealand that night, she might have talked sense into Dad and the whole horrendous thing might have ended there and then. But she wasn't there, and Javed was, and he was the one who twigged it in the end and gave us that one last chance of saving Dad from himself.

Mum left as planned on New Year's Day, and that afternoon Javed came round. Dad and I made a huge Sunday dinner, which we had early, then he went off to his office to do something or other and the boys cleared a space in the sitting room and did some aikido. They were out of practice, and the classes were due to start again the following Saturday.

The phone rang. Dad took it in the hall. I noticed that the boys had become harder and faster in their sparring. Before, it had been something like dancing. Now it was definitely fighting. They still had scrupulous manners and they never hurt each other, but I was in no doubt that they could have, if they'd wanted to.

Dad came in and sat on the arm of the sofa. 'That man's a basket case,' he said.

'Who?'

'Davenport. Look at the state of the world and all he can worry about is red squirrels.'

'What did he want?'

'Oh, the usual. How is it going and how much longer? But he's definitely losing it. He offered me a massive bonus if I can get it up and running before the end of the month.'

'How much?' said Alex.

'Oh, silly money,' said Dad. 'Enough to pay off the mortgage, anyway.'

'Enough to put up your chalet in the garden?' I said.

'Yes.'

'Enough to turn the shed into an aikido dojo?' said Alex.

'Yes,' said Dad.

'Wow,' I said. 'And can you do it?'

Dad shrugged. 'I don't know. It's in the lap of the gods at this stage.'

'But you're ready to test it, aren't you?'

'Nearly,' said Dad.

I remembered what he had said to Mum about having the final decision on whether to hand over the results.

'Will you take the money?' I said. 'If it works, I mean? Will you hand it over?'

The question stopped Dad in his tracks. I like to believe that just then, with all that was happening, he was ready to turn it down. I wanted to say something; to tell him that I believed in him, and that he was right, but I didn't get the chance. We all heard it at the same time and froze in alarm.

There was someone outside the house.

4

We could hear a man's voice, deep and strong, speaking in the darkness.

'What the hell . . .?' I said to Dad, but he stood glued to the spot like the rest of us, straining to hear. The voice went on, repeating something in a rhythmic, almost musical way. The walls of the house were too thick for us to hear what the words were.

Finally Dad moved and went towards the window.

'It's on the other side of the house, Dad,' said Alex. He and Javed raced out into the hall but Dad called them back.

'I'll go. You lot stay here.'

He went to the door and opened it. Instantly we could hear the voice perfectly.

'A measure of wheat for a penny. Three measures of barley for a penny.'

We ignored Dad's orders and crowded behind him in the hallway. All four of us stood and stared out.

'Mind you don't damage the oil and the wine.' They were standing at the edge of the orchard facing the house. The white horse, the red, and now a third one: huge and fat, and pure jet-black. It appeared to have no reins at all. Its head was down and it was tearing voraciously at the orchard grass. Its rider was fat as well, and in his hand he held an old-fashioned set of scales with two brass dishes hanging from a wooden cross bar.

'A measure of wheat for a penny . . .'

The voice was rich and coloured with self-satisfaction.

'Three measures of barley for a penny . . .'

Dad was under the spell already, I could tell by the look on his face. A January wind blew leaves into the hall.

'Mind you don't damage the oil and the wine.'

Alex and Javed, still in their hakamas, stepped past Dad and into the yard. A little less confidently, I followed.

'A measure of wheat for a penny.'

I wondered how it was that we could see them so clearly. It was pitch-dark in the orchard and the light from the house windows was nowhere near strong enough to show them in such clarity. Around them the trees were barely visible. It was as though they carried their own light within them.

'Three measures of barley . . .'

'What do they want?' Alex whispered to me, and at the same time Dad drifted up behind us, his steps slow and silent on the flagged yard.

'. . . for a penny.'

I caught Dad's arms as he passed, feeling exhausted suddenly; feeling like a minder whose patient had recovered and has suddenly relapsed. 'No, Dad,' I said. 'Not again.'

Javed and Alex turned to look at him. He had relaxed in my grasp, and was swaying lightly from foot to foot, as though he was hearing some glorious, ethereal music.

'Dad?' said Alex.

Dad sighed wistfully, and when we turned back the horsemen were gone. Javed made to move towards the orchard but I was shaking with fear. 'Leave it, Javed!'

'Who are they?' said Alex.

Dad was trembling, still staring at the empty orchard, like someone in the grip of a terrible conflict. I held on to his arm, but he wasn't going anywhere now.

'What was that?' said Alex. 'Who were they?'

'You see?' I said to him, my fear transforming into irrational fury. 'You didn't believe me!'

'I never said I didn't believe you!' he said.

'You did.'

'When?'

'You implied it anyway!'

'Girls, boys,' said Dad. His voice was dreamy and calm. He had stopped shaking. He was acting again. 'Stop squabbling.'

He turned and went into the house. Alex called after him, but he got no answer. The door slammed hard.

'You see?' I said. 'You see the way he is?'

We went in after him, but he was already coming back out through the hallway, his car keys in his hand.

'Where are you going?' said Alex.

'Got a few things to do in the lab,' said Dad cheerfully. 'Didn't I just promise you a dojo?'

'Wait, Dad,' I said. 'We have to talk about this.'

'Talk about what?' And he was gone, into the car and away into the night.

The boys and I wandered into the kitchen.

'What's going on?' said Javed.

I felt exhausted; shattered and defeated. 'I haven't a clue.'

'What was all that stuff about wheat and barley?' said Alex.

'He's like a market trader,' said Javed.

'Was he trying to sell us something?' I said.

'No,' said Javed. 'It was a message, though.'

'That's what I think,' I said. 'But what's he trying to tell us?'

The sound of the front doorbell made all three of us jump out of our skins. For several long moments we all stood rooted to the spot, then Javed took a deep breath and went to open it. It was Attiya.

'Are you all right?' she said to him. 'You look as if you've had a fright.'

'I'm fine,' said Javed.

She looked along the hallway at Alex and me. 'You

all look as if you were expecting trouble. Been watching a scary film?'

'Something like that,' said Alex.

While Javed changed out of his hakama, Alex and I sat in the kitchen with Attiya. She could tell that we were completely distracted, and I was tempted to blurt it all out. I don't know why I didn't; why neither of us did. Attiya was someone you could talk to about anything. But the horsemen and the effect they'd had on Dad was like a kind of guilty secret that all three of us now shared. And after they were gone, I felt certain that Javed wouldn't tell his mother anything either.

I turned on the TV, but we couldn't watch it. I went upstairs and Alex followed me to my room, still in his hakama, and sat on the floor.

'I'm sorry I didn't believe you,' he said.

'It doesn't matter. I don't blame you. I can hardly believe it myself.'

'Whatever it is, it's as scary as hell,' he said. 'I mean, I wasn't scared that they were going to do anything. It was just . . .'

'I know,' I said. 'They're not holograms.'

'No. They're not holograms.'

We fell silent, listening to the TV in the room below us. We should have turned it off, but the ordinary sounds were comforting in the empty house. When the phone rang it made us both jump. Alex raced down to answer it, and a minute later he was back, breathless with excitement. 'He's found them!'

'What?'

'Javed. He looked them up on the Internet. Have we got a Bible?'

'A Bible! What do we want with a Bible?'

Alex showed me the chapter and verse he'd written on the phone message pad. And as he did so I remembered the Bible I'd seen in Dad's study after he'd talked about science bringing atheists close to God. I ran down to see if it was still there. It was, buried under a pile of letters and bills. Alex took ages finding the place but he wouldn't let me do it. Eventually he found it, and read aloud:

'Revelation, Chapter Six:

And I saw when the Lamb opened one of the seals, and I heard, as it were the noise of thunder, one of the four beasts saying, Come and see.

And I saw, and behold a white horse and he that sat on him had a bow, and a crown was given unto him: and he went forth conquering and to conquer.

And when he had opened the second seal I heard the second beast say, Come and see.

And there went out another horse that was red: and power was given to him that sat thereon to take peace from the earth, and that they should kill one another: and there was given unto him a great sword.'

'That's it,' I said. 'That's our empire and rebellion. It practically says so!'

'And when he had opened the third seal I heard the third beast say, Come and see. And I beheld, and lo a black horse; and he that sat on him had a pair of balances in his hand.'

'Yes!'

'And I heard a voice in the midst of the four beasts say, A measure of wheat for a penny, and three measures of barley for a penny; and see thou hurt not the oil and the wine.

'And when he had opened the fourth seal I heard the voice of the fourth beast say, Come and see.

'And I looked, and behold a pale horse; and his name that sat on him was Death, and Hell followed with him. And power was given unto them over the fourth part of the earth, to kill with sword, and with hunger, and with death, and with the beasts of the earth.'

Alex glanced through the next few lines but didn't read on. 'That's all there is about the horsemen,' he said.

I nodded. 'That's who they are then.'

'Who are they?' said Alex.

I had never read that part of the Bible, but I had

heard of the horsemen. I thought everybody had. I was surprised that Alex didn't know.

'They're the four horsemen of the apocalypse,' I said. 'And when they appear it's supposed to mean the end of the world.'

PART FIVE

PART FIVE

1

Alex and I sat up talking in my room until the early hours. We heard Dad come in about midnight, whistling to himself as he came upstairs. We expected him to pop his head round the door, but he didn't; he just went straight to bed. We talked some more, trying to come up with a plan of action, but short of barricading Dad into his bedroom we couldn't think of anything. The problem was that we didn't really know what we were up against. We had seen the horsemen; we had looked right into their eyes; but we didn't know what had brought them there or what we could do to stop them. Eventually, stressed and exhausted, we both dropped off to sleep, still in our clothes.

I woke with one idea in my mind. We couldn't keep Dad here, but I could at least keep an eye on him. He was clearly going back to work on a serious basis, which meant that it was time for me to go back, too. I got dressed and went, bleary-eyed, down into the kitchen.

Dad had already finished with his breakfast.

'Go back to bed, sweetheart,' he said.

'I'm coming in to work,' I said.

'No need,' he said. 'I can manage on my own from here on in.'

'From here on in?' I said. 'How come? Have you finished?'

'Not yet. But I don't need an assistant any more.'

'You can't do that,' I said. 'You can't give me the sack, just like that.'

'You can have pay instead of notice,' he said. 'But I don't need you at the lab. I'll work better on my own.'

I shook my head. 'I don't know what's going on, Dad, but I think you're in trouble. I'm going to tell Mum this time.'

'Tell her what?'

'About the horsemen we saw last night, that's what!'

Dad laughed. 'And do you think she'll believe you? If I deny it?'

'Yes, I do. If Alex and Javed and me all swear to it.'

'To what? Visions in the night?'

I was shaking with rage when he left. Alex came down, fresh from the shower.

'I am going to tell Mum,' I told him. 'I don't care what he says. As soon as she phones I'm going to tell her.'

He made breakfast but neither of us had much of an appetite. While we were scraping the leftovers into the bin, Javed arrived on his bike. There were no preliminaries. It was a council of war from the word go.

He had been doing some more research on the Internet, and he knew a lot more than we did.

'They're definitely the horsemen of the apocalypse,' he said. 'But why were there only three?'

'Only three so far,' I said. 'There's obviously a pattern to it, isn't there? First one, then two, now three.'

'So we can expect the fourth one to be with them next time?' said Javed.

'Looks like it.'

'Which means curtains,' said Alex.

'That's what they say,' said Javed. 'That's what people mean when they talk about the apocalypse, anyway. The end of the world. I found loads of stuff on the Net about the four horsemen but it's not easy to work out what it means.'

'Stuff like what?' said Alex.

'Most of it is kind of religious commentaries and I didn't find them very helpful. The type of people who can't get out of the Christian mindset at all. They mostly say things like the white horseman is Christ and the red one is Death and the black one is corruption or famine or something. But I think we were closer to the mark.'

'It says he went forth conquering and to conquer,' said Alex.

'And when the red one comes along he takes peace from the world and they start killing each other. Which ties in with our theory of rebellion against the empire.'

'So what about the black horse then?' I said. 'What does he represent? Business interests?'

'That's what I think, anyway,' said Javed. 'The big companies that trade in arms and oil and stuff. They're behind a lot of what's happening in the world.'

'And his horse has no reins at all,' said Alex. 'He's completely out of control. Nobody's even trying to restrain him.'

'Corporate control of the global economy,' said Javed. 'The money behind the western governments that controls their foreign policy.'

'Maybe,' I said, disliking the idea even as I said it. 'Or maybe it's more simple. Maybe it's people being tempted to do things for money, even when they know it's wrong.'

'Your father,' said Javed.

Alex was appalled. 'He wouldn't, would he? He always says he does it because he loves the science of it.'

'He does,' I said. 'But maybe the money is an extra incentive.'

'I don't really need the dojo,' said Alex miserably. 'It was a joke really.'

'But where does it leave us, anyway?' said Javed. 'What's it telling us about your dad's work? We already know the other stuff. The world is a mess, anyone can see that.'

'The world's in a mess but it's not over until the fat lady sings,' said Alex.

'And who is the fat lady?' I asked.

'The fourth horseman,' said Alex. 'He's the key

to it all. We have to work out what he represents and try and find a way to stop him before he turns up.'

'And unleashes the apocalypse,' said Javed.

'Oh, this is crazy,' I said. 'Are you saying it's up to us to save the world?'

The boys went quiet and we listened to the wind driving rain against the window. Then Javed said, 'Should we just forget about it then? Pretend it never happened, like your dad does?'

'We have to focus on Dad,' said Alex. 'It's him they want, after all. And if it's all down to the last horseman, we have to find the connection.'

'*Behold a pale horse*,' I quoted. 'Why "pale"?'

'One of the commentaries on the Internet has something about that,' said Javed. 'Apparently in the original Hebrew the word means greenish or yellowish, the way someone looks if they're ill. They said it meant the pale horseman signified disease.'

'*And his name that sat on him was Death*,' I quoted.

'And no one could interpret what that last bit meant, about killing with the beasts of the earth.'

'But we can,' I said, an unpleasant realization sending prickles down my spine. 'This is where Dad comes in, isn't it?'

'That's what I think,' said Javed. 'The beasts of the earth used for experimentation with disease.'

'And then something goes wrong,' said Alex.

'It could happen,' said Javed. 'If a virus escaped, perhaps.'

I knew how careful Dad was and how thorough his precautions were. I also knew that viruses did sometimes escape from laboratories. In the 1970s a strain of smallpox had got out of the microbiology lab in Birmingham and a woman had died as a result. The security measures were much tighter now and there hadn't been a case of smallpox since, but anything was possible.

'But why Dad's lab?' I said. 'There are much more dangerous viruses all over the world. His one is only going to be harmful to squirrels, after all.'

'That's as far as we know,' said Alex. 'But what if it went wrong? Mutated or something? Like the bird flu, you know? It started off in birds then spread to humans.'

It seemed very plausible to me. I was sure that Alex had put his finger on it and that there was going to be some terrible mistake at the lab. I was wrong, though. There were no mistakes being made at the lab. Everything was working out exactly as Mr Davenport had intended it to.

2

I told the boys that I would talk to Dad about it that night. I was going to let him know that I was ready to start talking. I wasn't only going to tell Mum, I was going to tell anyone I thought might listen to me. I would even go to the police if I had to, or the mayor of Worcester. I was going to spill the beans on his project because I believed it was dangerous and he ought to close it down, chalet or no chalet. I wasn't going anywhere and I was prepared to wait up as long as I needed to.

The trouble was, he didn't come back.

Alex had volunteered to join me, but in the end he had gone home with Javed for the night. I said that was fine and I didn't need any help, but as the minutes and hours ticked by I began to wish that he had stayed.

I tried to phone the lab but I knew it was useless. Dad took the phone off the hook when he was busy with intricate work, and he couldn't take the mobile into the inner lab because it couldn't go through the shower with him. At ten o'clock I tried it anyway, in case he was on his way home. It rang, but there was no answer.

I waited another half-hour then tried both numbers again. What bothered me was that even if he was going to be a bit late he always phoned to let us know, especially if Mum was away. I began to imagine terrible scenes at the lab. What if the virus had mutated and attacked him? What if he was ill and couldn't get to the phone? Or what if the horsemen had turned up again; all four of them this time?

I rang Alex to see if Dad had called him, but he hadn't. Alex was alarmed now as well, and he suggested we go over to the lab and find out what was happening. But it was a dark, wild night out there, far too stormy for us to go by bike.

'What about Attiya?' I said. 'Would she take us?'

'She's been in bed since nine o'clock,' said Alex. 'She always goes to bed early because she gets up at five.'

'Couldn't you wake her?'

Alex chatted to Javed for a moment, then came back on the line. 'Javed says we should get a taxi.'

It was good thinking. I phoned one of the city-based companies and gave them the address of the Maliks' house. Twenty minutes later the taxi arrived at my door, with the boys in the back.

When we got to the lab we asked the driver to wait, but he wanted the money for the journey so far before he would agree. I don't blame him. We were outside a gate in the middle of nowhere in the middle of the night. I gave him a twenty-pound note and told him to hold on to the change until we got back. That surprised him.

'What you up to anyway?' he said.

'Looking for our dad,' I said.

The driver glanced at Javed and it was clear that he didn't believe us.

'We're not up to mischief,' I told him.

'Just wait,' said Javed, with the assurance of someone who had grown up giving orders.

We didn't think of checking to see whether Dad's car was in the barn. A high wind was pelting us with stinging rain, and we just ran straight for the buildings. I let us in and felt Javed shudder at the scurry of rodent feet in the cage room. I turned on the lights and did a quick count of the squirrels in the cages. There were only eleven left.

'Dad?' I called through the intercom. There was no answer.

'He must have gone home,' said Alex, his voice small and anxious.

'Then why isn't he there?'

'Maybe he went somewhere else. For a pint or something.'

Dad was fond of a glass of wine but he never, as far as I knew, went to the pub.

'I'm going in,' I said. 'Tell the taxi to wait a bit longer, will you?'

Javed ran off and I opened the door into the bug-lock. I should have known the minute I got in that Dad wasn't there, but I wasn't thinking straight. I'd never been through before and I hadn't got used to the drill. Even when I took my clothes off and hung them on the empty pegs it didn't cross my mind that if Dad had been inside his clothes would have been hanging there as well. I felt horribly vulnerable as I stepped, naked, into the shower. There were all kinds of disinfectants in there and I scrubbed myself with pretty much everything and washed my hair three times. On the other side of the shower cubicle there were white suits like hospital robes hanging on more pegs. There were new ones in polythene as well, stacked on a shelf, so I opened one of those and dressed myself, and put on one of the surgical masks that I found beside them.

That was when it occurred to me that I could be making a terrible mistake. What if the worst of my imaginings turned out to be reality? What if a virus had somehow mutated and had attacked Dad? The pictures that assailed my mind were almost unbearable. I imagined Dad lying dead on the floor, or shaking in the final stages of a dreadful fever. A new terror struck me as I realized that going in there might be the worst thing I could do. If Dad was ill, or dead, then I might get the virus as well. I might die, and if I didn't, and I left the lab, then I might give the disease to everyone else, and it might spread across the whole country.

I was in a lather of sweat by now. There was an intercom in the virus room but none in the bug-lock. I couldn't contact the boys for advice. I was on my own. I looked down at myself, dressed in the crisp new suit. It seemed ridiculous. Dressing like that didn't make me a doctor or a scientist. I was completely unequipped. This wasn't a job for me. It was something for the police or the army or the special services. The trouble was, none of those people were here. I could go out and call someone, blow the whistle on the whole project as I had threatened to do. Perhaps I should have done. Perhaps everything would have worked out better if I had.

I don't know what it was that decided me, in the end. I like to think it was the warrior spirit emerging, but maybe it wasn't that. Maybe it was just stupidity or recklessness. But I was alone at the crease. The ball was there to be played. I made my decision instinctively, and I played it. I went into the lab.

Dad was neither dead nor dying. He wasn't there at all. I waited a moment or two to allow the huge sense of relief to sink in, then I looked around. The chaos surprised me. The computer desk was piled high with papers, journals, books, coffee cups. The waste bin was overflowing with printouts and biscuit wrappers. There was a bag of squirrel food overflowing in a corner, but no sign of squirrels.

I went further in. Along the far wall was a row of machines: electron microscopes, incubators, that kind of thing. I knew their names from hearing Dad talk about them, but I didn't know which was which. There was a steel sink, and above it was a shelf of chemicals, flasks, syringes and other things I didn't recognize. At the end of the bench were two other doors, side by side. The first one I opened led into a tiny kitchen with another door leading into a toilet cubicle. The whole place had Dad's familiar ashtray smell about it and I backed out. There was nothing to see in there.

The other door had some kind of seal, soft and strong. It hissed when I pushed it open. There was another small room behind it, only about three metres square. The rest of the squirrels were in there; ten of them, five red and five grey. All the red ones bounded up the mesh walls, delighted to see me coming. But all my little greys, my Garys and Gooches and Gitas, were lying dead and stone-cold in the bottom of their cage.

I was still staring at them, trying to work out the implications of what I was seeing, when I heard the noise of the bug-lock door opening. I jumped, afraid it was Dad, or something worse like a troop of horsemen. But it was the boys, both dressed like me in the surgical suits.

'What's happening?' Alex asked.

'He's done it,' I said. They joined me in the second doorway and stared, like me, at the dead squirrels.

'My God,' said Alex. 'It's worked.'

Javed looked at us both but said nothing. He turned and began looking around the main lab, reading bits of documents and scrutinizing the machines.

'Dad's not here anyway,' said Alex.

We went out through the bug-lock, one after another. It took ages, and by the time we were all back in our own clothes and had the lab locked up it was nearly midnight. The taxi driver, decent man, had waited all that time. I got him to go to Javed's house first, and on the way there Alex decided that he'd come home with me to see if we could track down Dad.

His car was outside the house. He was up in bed with the light out. But Alex and I had no qualms about disturbing him.

He wasn't asleep. 'Hello, you two,' he said. 'Had a good evening?'

'No,' I said. 'We haven't. We've just come back from the lab.'

'From the lab?' He sat up in bed. 'What on earth were you doing there?'

'We were looking for you! Where were you?'

'I came straight back here. I must have passed you on the road or something. How did you get there?'

I told him, and I told him what we had seen. He couldn't contain his delight. 'It worked better than I ever expected,' he said. 'Just perfect. I know how you feel about the squirrels, sweetheart, but I promise you they hardly knew what hit them. It was so quick.'

'It's not the squirrels. It's . . .'

'What?'

'The horsemen,' said Alex. 'There's something badly

wrong about all this. You can't go on with it, Dad.'

'But there's nowhere else to go with it,' Dad said. 'I'm handing it all over to Mr Davenport tomorrow, and he's going to hand me a big, fat bank draft. And that'll be the end of it.'

'You can't. To hell with the dojo and the chalet. You can't do this.'

'Listen,' said Dad. 'You know I've had reservations about it myself. But I had a long, long chat with Mr Davenport this evening. He told me they have no intention of setting this thing loose all over the country. They're going to do a controlled trial on an offshore island before they even think about doing anything else. There can't possibly be any harm in that, can there?'

I couldn't see how there could be, but I wasn't about to give up, and nor was Alex. 'What about the horsemen? You know who they were, don't you? You know what it means if the last one turns up with them?'

Dad sighed deeply. 'We'll talk about that some time. After tomorrow I'll have all the time in the world. It's going to be great. Maybe we'll even go to India with your mum.'

'I don't want to go to India,' I said. 'I want . . .'

But I no longer knew what I wanted. The lab was going to be closed down anyway. Nothing could happen that hadn't already happened, and the fourth horseman hadn't appeared.

Yet.

'Look,' he said. 'Can we talk about this tomorrow morning? I'm tired. And you two should be congratulating me instead of dragging me over the coals. I've done what I set out to do. I've achieved something that has never been done before.'

Maybe it was churlish, but I said it anyway. 'Well done. The scientific colossus, bestriding the world.'

It gives me the creeps now, thinking about that. I had no idea what I was saying.

3

I woke to the sound of Dad's car driving away from the house. For a moment everything seemed fine. I was just turning over to go back to sleep again when I remembered. I was jolted awake and I jumped straight out of bed.

'Alex!'

By the time I came out of the bathroom he was standing at his bedroom door in his pyjamas. They were old ones. The trouser legs were too short.

'What's up?'

'Dad's already gone. To meet Mr Davenport. He didn't wait for us to get a chance to talk to him.'

Alex swore. 'We'll just go after him,' he said. 'He's going to have to listen to us.'

But I was no clearer this morning than I had been the previous night. I wasn't sure what it was that we had to stop. It was all over, wasn't it? That's what Dad had said. So what was there left for us to do? Should we stop him handing over the information and getting his money?

I went downstairs and stood in the middle of the kitchen, trying to work it out. Alex came down, still in his pyjamas, looking similarly bewildered.

'What exactly are we going to do?' he said.

But everything was about to become clear. We

hadn't worked it out, but Javed had. He came skidding into the yard and dropped his bike on the flagstones. We went out to meet him, but for a moment or two he was panting so hard that he couldn't even speak. Finally he managed a single, breathless word.

'Genocide.'

'What?'

He gulped in air. 'That's what your dad's done. He has written a recipe for genocide.'

Alex and I just gaped at him, and he had to struggle on. 'Just one tiny genetic difference. One vital kind of cell, that's all it takes. If it can be done with animals . . .'

'It can be done with humans,' Alex finished up.

'A disease that can kill me and not you,' said Javed. 'Or you and not me. If it gets into the wrong hands . . .'

I was already racing for my bike. Everything was falling into place. All the secrecy, the mobile numbers that kept changing, and above all, the horsemen. And I was quite certain that the information was already on its way into the wrong hands. I knew now what it was that we had to stop.

The three of us pedalled for our lives. Or if not for our lives, for the lives of millions of others who might die if Mr Davenport got his hands on the project records that Dad had made. Poor Alex was barefooted, still in pyjamas. People in cars stared at him as they passed us, but we had worse things to worry about than that. None of us had watches, but we must have covered those four miles in fifteen minutes or less. We were all gasping for breath when we pulled up outside the gates. Dad was standing there, staring at us in amazement. He had a flask and a box file in his hands. At his feet, concealed from the road by a tangle of dead brambles, was a green plastic coolbox.

'What are you lot doing here?' he said. He seemed to be looking at us, but he wasn't, not quite. He was staring straight through us. I had seen that look on his face before. It frightened me witless.

'You said you would talk to us, Dad. You promised.'

'I didn't want to wake you,' he said, his voice flat, toneless. Acting again. Acting badly. 'You wouldn't have appreciated it.' He bent down and put the flask and the file into the coolbox, then he looked at Alex. 'Why on earth are you in your pyjamas?'

Alex ignored the question. 'What's in the coolbox?' he said.

'Never mind what's in it now,' said Dad, and there was a cold light in his eyes as he spoke. 'It's a magic box. When you next look into it there'll be a dojo in it!'

We all looked at the box.

'Why the big mystery?' I said. 'Why can't you just hand it to Davenport?'

'He's not sure how long he'll be,' said Dad. 'I don't want to be hanging around here waiting for him all morning. I have . . .' He hesitated. 'I have somewhere I have to go.' He nodded in the direction of the buildings and I could see a shimmer of heat distorting the air above the chimney. I wondered what he had been burning.

'You can't hand that stuff over, Dad,' said Alex.

'I don't know what's wrong with you kids!' Dad looked at his watch and walked back through the open gates. We followed him down the drive towards the buildings, but we didn't make it as far as the lab. Dad stopped on the drive which ran between the buildings and the woodland. We followed his gaze.

They were back.

And I looked, and behold a pale horse.

All four horses were there now. The white, the red, the black, and an awful, sickly-looking creature with a huge, skeletal head that hung at the end of a bony neck, only a whisker above the ground. It wasn't white or grey or cream. It was pale, with the faint yellow-green hues of fading bruises, or of pus. But the worst thing about it, the thing that froze our blood in our veins, was that it was riderless. The other three horsemen had brought it with them, saddled and ready to be ridden by the fourth. They had come to collect Dad.

And he was ready to go. He was beginning to move towards that horrendous creature as though he was without any choice in the matter. And perhaps he was. He had been under the spell of the horsemen since he had made the decision to pursue his fatal research. He had broken away from them for a short time, when the crisis happened in Shasakstan, but they had over-powered him again, that night when Mr Davenport phoned. And now the pale horse was his to ride as the horsemen drew the apocalypse down upon the human race.

But we still had choice.

'No!' Alex hurled himself at Dad, grabbing him by the arm and swinging him round.

'Hold him,' said Javed, and he made an elegant, twisting motion that looked like an aikido move. Alex nodded and, without hesitating, curled a leg round Dad's knee and dropped him to the ground, then pinned him there with a simple arm-lock.

Javed was already haring down the drive towards the gate, and a moment later he was back, the box file in one hand and the steel flask in the other.

'Come on,' he said to me, running back towards the door to the lab. 'It all has to go. Everything.'

For a moment I was paralysed, staring at the awful sights ahead of me. The horsemen, with that dreadful, deathly creature, and on the drive a few metres away, another nightmare. Dad was struggling desperately in Alex's aikido hold and making the most awful noise. If he'd been shouting or swearing I could have handled it better, but he was wailing, pleading with Alex as though his life depended on it. His whole body was heaving with the effort to escape. I was amazed that Alex could hold him.

'Come on!' Javed yelled.

I wanted to run away, deny what was happening. What changed my mind was a twinge in my elbow, like an echo of a time when I had made the wrong decision. I remembered what Attiya had said. 'Sometimes you have to run away, as fast as you can.' But this wasn't one of those times. What was happening now had to be faced. I moved at last; ran ahead of Javed and unlocked the door. He sprinted through and made straight for the bug-lock. While I waited for him to go through the shower I found a pair of tiny wire nippers. One by one I took the squirrels out of their cages, removed their ear tags and dropped them into the transport cages. When I was finished I had eleven ear tags. Eleven squirrels left, in two small cages. They didn't like the enclosed space, and several squabbles had already started. I put the ear tags into my pocket and left them to it.

By the time I was showered and suited, Javed had already done a phenomenal amount of damage in the lab. All the machines were in a broken heap on the floor, and reams of printer paper were scattered around and over them. At the top of the pile were the box file and the flask.

I headed straight for the back room, expecting to find the red squirrels still alive in there, but they were gone. Of course they were. Dad, scrupulous to the last, could never have brought them back through the bug-lock. They would have carried the virus into the cage room, from where it could have gone anywhere. So that was what he had been burning that morning. Carcasses.

'A light,' said Javed. He was sprinkling pure alcohol from brown bottles on top of the paper. 'We need a light.'

We stood there, looking and feeling foolish. The world on the verge of disaster for want of a match. Javed began rummaging in drawers, but I remembered something. A smell. Like an ashtray.

'Javed, go out. Go back through the shower.'

'Are you nuts? Take a shower now?'

'It's more important than ever now. There's no point in doing all this if we bring the virus out with us.'

'But how are you going to light it?'

I went into the little kitchen. I knew Dad couldn't bring cigarettes and lighters through every time he came in, and that he would have a stash somewhere. It was in the first drawer I opened. Two cartons of cigarettes and four coloured lighters. I held one up so Javed could see.

'Now go!'

'You go,' he said. 'I'll light it and come after you.'

But this was my job. On that day in early summer when I'd decided to be a warrior, my fate was already pointing to this moment. I thought I had been abandoned by my courage when I didn't go to Shasakstan with Alex and Javed, but I hadn't. It had nothing to do with Shasakstan. It was about this. I didn't know it then, but I was certain of it now. Javed must have understood it too, because he didn't hesitate any longer. He left.

I waited. It seemed like an eternity.

Outside, Alex told me later, Dad was pleading with him to let him get up. He swore blind he wouldn't do anything and, finally, Alex was persuaded to trust him. He let go of the arm-lock and Dad got up. Alex said he was deranged. He ran towards that awful horse first, and then he doubled back and began to race towards the lab. Alex had no choice but to bring him down again, with a rugby tackle this time. That was when Dad hit his head.

I gave Javed time to get through the bug-lock, and then I waited for a few moments longer. I'll never be able to properly describe what I felt during that time. I was besieged by doubt. The weight of the responsibility that was on me was almost more than I could stand. I had to keep still. I had to keep my mind from darting like the flies in the cool shadows beneath the trees. It wanted to escape from the truth, to believe in Dad and the squirrels and the dojo. It wanted to be a child's mind again, free of the dreadful responsibility that Javed's realization had brought upon us. I couldn't let it. I had to wait until certainty arrived and stopped my hand from shaking. I saw it first from a distance, bouncing towards me across the rough turf of time. Dad couldn't stop it. Mr Davenport couldn't stop it. The horsemen couldn't stop it. It sped up as it came.

I took it cleanly, calmly, and flicked the lighter. Just once. The tiny flame touched one of the alcohol-soaked pages. There was a little trickle of blue flame and then the whole lot went up in an instant inferno. I opened the door, dived through it into the bug-lock and slammed it behind me.

I was already in the shower before I realized I still had the cigarette lighter in my hand. I didn't know what to do with it. I was terrified and desperate to get out before the fire became too strong. It was ridiculous, one of those small absurdities, like Alex being in pyjamas, that mocked the seriousness of the situation. In the time I had, the best I could think of was to wash it as well. I drenched it in disinfectant and brought it through to the other side.

By the time I got there, smoke was already leaking through the partition wall into the kitchen corridor. In the cage room the squirrels could smell it. They were frantic in their confined space, but they wouldn't have to worry for much longer. I grabbed one cage in each hand and ran with them, out of the door and into the yard.

Javed was waiting for me. We raced for the trees, and when we turned we could see flames leaping skywards, and a huge column of smoke rising up into the atmosphere. It would be seen from miles away.

Dad was lying on his back on the gravel and Alex was bending over him. I opened the cages and tipped the squirrels out on to the grass. They scattered, racing in all directions, but I didn't wait to see where they went. I joined Alex and Javed at Dad's side, and stayed there, trying to wake him.

Under the trees, the horsemen were still there, but shifting restlessly now, as though they were anxious to leave. As we watched, the pale, ghastly horse staggered and shuddered and, with a huge effort, raised its cadaverous head. For a long moment it stared at us through dim, milky eyes. Then it, along with the others, vanished.

❧ 4 ❧

It took ages for them to find me an appropriate adult; a social worker from Warndon. After that we had to get a duty solicitor. While I was waiting, PC Courtney came in to tell me that they'd got the report from the hospital. Dad had concussion, but nothing worse. He was rambling a bit, she said, and they were going to keep him under observation until he improved. But there was nothing to worry about. No long-term damage.

Not to his brain perhaps, I thought. But I wasn't so sure about his mind. We were all going to have to go through some readjustment, and him more than any of us.

'What happened to him anyway?' she asked.

'He fell,' I said.

I had been in the interview room for about twenty minutes when we were interrupted. In that time I had said ten words to them.

'Do you know what your friendly neighbourhood scientist is doing?'

They had taken that as a reason to pursue the animal rights line, but I hadn't said anything else. Not a single word. And I haven't since. I haven't had to. The officer who interrupted our session brought the news that the cases had all been dropped. There were exclamations of astonishment and a brief but futile argument outside the door of the interview room, but it was all over. They must have traced the ownership of the building to somewhere higher up, and they must have been ordered to drop the charges . . .

As Javed knew they would. He had figured it all out. The people behind the project would not want any prosecutions brought. A case against Javed and me would bring Dad's work out into the open. There would be investigations, perhaps even an enquiry. Far better for Mr Davenport and his colleagues to quietly admit defeat and vanish back into the musty woodwork of their secretive ministry in the back corridors of Whitehall.

Because it was someone from our government. It had to have been. It required a powerful influence to get a criminal case dropped as quickly as that. We'll never know who, though, because 'Mr Davenport' kept his tracks too well covered.

Perhaps it was just meant as a threat, like nuclear weapons have been for the last sixty years. Perhaps they would never have used it. But Javed and Alex and I believe that they would have done. What other reason could there have been for the sudden urgency, the huge bribe, coming so soon after the crisis in Shasakstan? And what other reason could there have been for that dreadful, diseased creature to come looking for its rider?

* * *

We'll never be sure, of course. But we do know this. If the pale horse had been ridden that day, a tide would have been unleashed that no one, not even Davenport and his employers, could have turned back.

5

We never did tell Mum or Attiya about the horsemen. What would have been the point? They would never have believed us. We told them the rest, though. Attiya says we ought to go public and get the people behind it out into the open, but Mum disagrees. She says they're too well protected, and we would only be opening up a can of worms for ourselves, particularly after what Javed and I had done. I think it's more than that, though. I think she's afraid of what might happen to all of us, if we started to pursue that kind of person. I think I am too.

Dad's getting better, but he's a shadow of his former self. His mind is recovering, though he never talks about the horsemen. He views Alex and me with a wary eye, as though he is afraid that we will confirm that the nightmare really happened. We stay quiet, and pretend he's just the same to us as he always was; our dad, our hero and role model. We all know it isn't true. His confidence has been so badly shaken that it will be some time before he thinks about getting any kind of work, so Mum has given up her job with the England team and has opened a private practice in Worcester. It's paying the mortgage, which is just as well. There was, of course, no bank draft. I wonder whether there would have been, even if the pick-up had been successful. So no outside office for Dad. No dojo for Alex. Oddly enough, we can live quite happily without them.

Manir hasn't come home, but Attiya did get a letter from him, smuggled into India by a friend and posted from there. He was well when he wrote it, and keeping out of trouble. He missed them all terribly and promised he'd see them before long. I was touched when I heard that he had remembered to send his love to us.

Alex and Javed are still best mates, but for some reason I've lost the desire to hang around with them so much. I can't see now why I ever wanted to. But sometimes, in rare, quiet moments, that strange bond is still there. The thing that we were destined to do is done. But we did our growing up together, and that isn't something that people ever forget. Especially when it's done all at once like that, on a single January morning.

I suppose I've changed as well. I've no job and no friends to speak of, but when you've looked into the eye of the apocalypse it's very hard to keep on feeling sorry for yourself. I'm well on the way to getting a life. I've been put back into centre forward on the hockey team. I've started aikido, and I love it. And, although it's still midwinter, I've put my name back on the cricket club list. I'm practising with Mum when the weather's good, and I'm practising on my own with a soft ball against the wall when it's not. All of a sudden I have no problem watching that ball, right on to the bat. I just can't wait for the season to start.

The situation in Shasakstan still hasn't been resolved. The Americans won't admit it, but everyone knows they are changing their policies. Strategic talks are being held. Attiya says they'll cut a deal. She says the tide has turned and things will begin to change, but not everyone is so optimistic. Some say the extremists are rallying in Shasakstan and elsewhere, and it will only be a matter of time before they raise a significant army and begin to spread their influence outwards from there. Perhaps they will. Perhaps they'll even become the next world empire, the next white horseman. Their business interests might displace the American and European ones. But whatever happens, they will meet with resistance. That's the nature of things. The white horseman has been striding through the world for thousands of years, with the red one and the black one at his side.

I think about them all the time, those horsemen, and I wonder who will, eventually, ride the pale horse? I know for certain that Dad wasn't the only person working in that dreadful field of endeavour. It's no secret that there are people out there trying to make viruses that will kill people of one race and not another. I often wonder whether they know what they're doing, or whether they are like Dad was, under the grip of some power that they don't understand. I hope they fail or, better still, come to their senses. Because as long as that awful pale horse remains riderless, the apocalypse will stay where it belongs.

Somewhere in the future.

Have you read about JJ's encounter with Irish music, myth and magic in Kate Thompson's award-winning novel, *The New Policeman*? JJ's story continues in her fantastic new book, *The Last of the High Kings*.

Turn over to read the opening pages . . .

On top of the mountain stood a hill of stones. It measured one hundred paces around the base and twenty paces from the bottom to the top. Of all the people of the seven tribes there was no one who could remember when it had been built, but of all the people of the seven tribes there was no one who could not remember why.

On top of the hill of stones stood a boy. He was barely twelve years old but he considered himself a man, already a proven warrior and hunter. If the talks going on in his father's fort went well he would soon be married. If they went badly he would, even sooner, be dead.

The young man who stood beside him on the hill of stones was a cousin. He was short; barely taller than the boy, and some people said it was his small size that had made him so angry. He was the right man to go hunting with and the wrong man to have an argument with. He had killed stags and bears and men in close combat, and when he saw blood he always wanted to see more of it. But even he had not wanted to see this blood; the blood of his young cousin. It was with great reluctance that he had allowed himself to be persuaded to take on this watch.

Throughout the whole of the night the two of them had waited on the beacon, taking it in turns to rest, but never to sleep. A constant hard wind had been blowing against them but it hadn't been that which kept them awake. They were watching for a messenger to tell them that the boy would live or a sign to tell them he would die.

Time after time, throughout that longest of nights, the boy wondered what had compelled him to speak. His father, as everyone had known he would, had asked for a hero, and the words were barely out of his mouth before the boy had called out with his own name. He hadn't thought about it. Something in him that was quicker and deeper than thought had spoken. The meeting had exploded into uproar. A dozen men and women demanded to be chosen instead of the boy and the voice that shouted loudest and longest was that of the man who stood beside him now. But it was no use. Battling against his own powerful feelings, the boy's father had quelled the storm. It was he who would be leading the forthcoming negotiations. It was right that his own flesh and blood should pay the price if they failed.

The fort on the edge of the plain could not be seen from the beacon, which was why two signalmen had been stationed at the edge of the mountain top. Both the fort and the mountain's edge had brush pyres waiting to be lit if the talks broke down. The one at the fort would signal to the watchers on the mountain and theirs, in turn, would signal to the boy. All through the night he had stared in its direction, sometimes imagining he saw the red glow of fire or smelled the smoke from burning kindling. Now, as the day dawned, he could see the two men, more cousins, their backs turned towards him as they kept their careful watch upon the fort. In the daylight the fires would not be lit. There were other signals instead. Arms stretched up and held still for success and reprieve. Arms to the sides and then up, waving, for failure and death.

The boy wondered why it was all taking so long. Could they still be talking down there? Perhaps the meeting had finished hours ago and no one had thought of coming up to tell them. He sighed and stamped his sandalled feet in an effort to warm them.

'Hungry?' said his cousin.

'No.'

There was bread and cold meat in a hide bag but

neither of them had touched it all night. The boy rewrapped his cloak around him and fastened it with the gold pin that his mother had given him shortly before her death.

'You keep this,' he said. 'If—'

But the young man shook his head. 'If you die I will not be long coming after you. There are those who say I'm an angry man, but if I am made to spill your blood there isn't a beast in the forest nor a man among the seven tribes that will not know what my anger looks like.'

The boy shook his head. 'Don't take it out on them,' he said. 'They aren't to blame for this.'

But he saw, already, the glint of derangement in those dark brown eyes, and he realized that an early death had always been written on his cousin's brow. And at that same moment he saw that the same thing was written on his own. His death was waving at him from the horizon. He saw the signallers turn back and look towards the plain, then wave again, more urgently.

'Do it,' he told his cousin.

'Then say it.' The boy looked and saw tears streaming down his cousin's wind-burned face. He turned away from him and saw the signalmen running hard, in opposite directions, away from their unlit pyre.

Something was coming. Already. How could it all

have happened so fast? The boy found that his knees were shaking so hard that they would scarcely support his weight.

'I swear,' he began, but his voice was constricted by fear and it squeaked like a child's. The words would be worthless if he did not mean them.

The mountain was shaking. Huge, heavy feet were thundering up the hillside from the plain.

'Say it,' said his cousin.

Two enormous, monstrous heads appeared over the rim of the mountain top, then a third, then a fourth. The creatures had reached the top and were advancing on the beacon with massive strides, and they were far, far more terrible than he had ever imagined.

There was no more time. The boy took a deep breath and, as he did so, all doubt left him.

'I swear that I will guard this place,' he said, and his voice was clear and strong. 'I will stay here and guard it whether I am alive or dead.'

The beasts were almost upon them. Behind him, the boy heard the whistling swish of a sword being swung through the air with ferocious strength.

And for a short while afterwards, everything was very, very still.

NEW YEAR'S EVE

NEW YEAR'S EVE

1

JJ Liddy stood in the hall and yelled at the top of his voice.

'Where's Jenny?'

The old house, which had been full of noise and activity, fell silent and still. JJ groaned, then shouted again.

'Has anybody seen Jenny?'

His wife, Aisling, came out of the sitting room. 'I thought you were watching her,' she said.

'Well, I was, a minute ago,' said JJ. 'Then I couldn't because she wasn't there.'

Aisling gave a martyred sigh. Their eldest, Hazel, appeared at the top of the stairs. 'She's not up here,' she said.

JJ went out into the yard. 'Jenny!' he yelled, trying to keep the irritation out of his voice. If she knew that he was angry she would never come. 'Jenny!'

She probably wouldn't come anyway. She rarely did.

JJ went back into the house and began searching for his walking boots. He found them underneath a pile of cased instruments which were waiting beside the door to be packed into the car, and as he was putting them on Donal came down the stairs with a half-filled backpack.

'Does that mean we aren't going, then?' he said. Donal was nine, and was by far the easiest of all Aisling and JJ's children. He seldom had much to say, and he never made a fuss about anything.

'Well, we can hardly go without her, can we?' said JJ, tugging at a bootlace.

'I don't see why not,' said Hazel, who was still at the top of the stairs, leaning on the banisters. 'I don't see why we have to let her ruin everything all the time.'

'Bold Jenny,' said Aidan, arriving on the scene with a hammer. He was going through an aggressive phase and Aisling and JJ spent a lot of their time trying to disarm him.

'She wouldn't care anyway,' Hazel went on. 'She doesn't want to hang around with the rest of us; that's why she's always swanning off on her own. She probably wouldn't even notice if we weren't here when she got back. She'd probably be delighted.'

'Oh, it doesn't matter,' said Aisling gloomily. 'We can always go in the morning.'

'It does matter,' said Hazel irritably. 'If we go in the

morning we'll miss the party, and that's the whole point.'

'I'll find her,' said JJ, lacing his second boot.

'Yeah, right you will,' said Hazel, stomping back to her bedroom.

JJ went out and shut the door behind him.

'Bold Daddy!' said Aidan, raising the hammer with both hands and aiming it at one of the glass panels in the door. Aisling snatched it out of his hand the instant before it hit the target and held it up high, out of his reach. He lunged at her and screamed, but she sidestepped and escaped into the kitchen. Silently, Donal retreated, leaving Aidan to finish his tantrum alone on the hallway floor.

As JJ crossed the field called Molly's Place he felt his annoyance subsiding. More than that, he found he could almost sympathize with Jenny. Although it was midwinter the weather was mild. A gentle breeze blew a soft, misty drizzle in from the sea, and the grey hills which rose ahead of him were inviting. Why would anyone want to squeeze into a crowded car and be stuck there for three hours when they could stride off into the fresh, earth-scented wilds beyond the farm?

He spotted something in the grass and changed his course. One of Jenny's shoes. It meant he was on the right track, at least. He looked up and caught a glimpse of something white on the mountainside far ahead. That big old goat again. It had been hanging around a lot lately, and it made JJ uneasy. He suspected that it might not be quite what it appeared to be. He suspected, as well, that Jenny was already a long, long way ahead. She hadn't got that much of a head start, he was fairly sure, but she was capable of moving incredibly quickly once she had, as she always did, jettisoned her shoes.

JJ looked at his watch. It was two o'clock, which meant that there were still about three hours of daylight left in which to find her. They wouldn't make it for dinner, but provided they were on the road by six they would still arrive in plenty of time for the party. His sister Marian had married an accordion player from Cork and their new year parties were famous in traditional music circles. They were one of the highlights of JJ's year, and the annual trip to Cork was just about the only time the whole family went away together. Everyone loved it and looked forward to it. Everyone, that was, except Jenny.

JJ found the other shoe just inside the boundary wall of the farm. That was good luck. More often than not only one would turn up, and Jenny's room was littered with shoes that had lost their partners.

'Jenny!'

Beyond the farm the land became much wilder. This

was the winterage that belonged to the Liddy farm, but unlike Mikey's land at the top of the mountain it had hardly any grazing at any time of year, and to a farmer it was useless. The rocky slopes rose steeply, and in hollows and gullies there were belts of woodland, mostly ash and hazel, guarded by blackthorn and brambles. There were plenty of places where Jenny could be hidden from view. She could be almost anywhere.

'Jenny!'

There was no answer. Even the white goat had disappeared. JJ sighed and, with a last glance back at the house, climbed over the dry-stone wall.

2

'Can I go to Ennis with the girls, then,' said Hazel, 'if Jenny's not back by six?'

'I suppose so,' said Aisling. It was nearly five already, and a few minutes earlier she had got up to turn on the outside light. This was not for JJ's benefit, or for Jenny's, but for Aidan, who had found three large pieces of polystyrene packaging in the shed and was out in the back yard, pulverizing them with a brick. It was making a terrible mess, which someone would have to clear up at some stage, but it was rare for anything to keep Aidan occupied for more than a couple of minutes at a time, and Aisling was reluctant to bring an end to the relative peace.

Hazel went off to phone her friends and book a seat on the bus. Aisling looked at the clock again. She would soon have to think about making a meal. There was hardly anything in the house, because they hadn't planned on being there that night. She could probably

269

scrape something together with tins and frozen food, but the trouble was she didn't want to. She had been looking forward to getting away; to being fed for a change, and to mucking in with Marian and Danny in the big friendly kitchen down in Cork. She had been looking forward to sitting at the piano and having a few tunes tonight. But then Jenny . . .

A wave of anxiety washed over her thoughts and changed their direction. What were they going to do about her? The child had been a disaster right from the word go. She wasn't stupid or devious or nasty, she was just completely intractable. She spent most of her time roaming around the countryside and seemed to be incapable of doing as she was told. And recently it had got worse. Much worse.

At least, in the past, she had gone to school. She still did occasionally, but it was becoming the exception rather than the rule. Most mornings when Aisling and JJ got up, Jenny was already gone. And when she was gone, she was gone all day. The girl didn't seem to need the things that normal children did. She never took anything to eat, and she never came home for lunch. She wore light clothes, often forgetting to take a jacket, even in the foulest of weather. And although Aisling's notes to the teachers were full of them, the truth was that Jenny never ever got a cough or a cold or a sore throat. But it couldn't go on. The school principal was beginning to get suspicious and had starting asking questions that Aisling found difficult to answer. It should have been JJ's responsibility to deal with that kind of thing, but the trouble was that JJ was hardly ever there.

Because JJ Liddy, over the last few years, had become a household name. He had made four CDs and he spent a large part of every year touring at home and abroad, playing to packed houses wherever he went. That hadn't been the plan when they married. The deal had been that JJ would stay at home and make violins, and Aisling would go back to working as a homoeopath. They were supposed to be sharing the housework and the child-rearing, but as the years went by, those things had become, almost exclusively, Aisling's department.

Anger simmered under her breastbone. She had put up with it for years, partly for the sake of JJ's career and partly because he was better paid for playing music than she would be for working as a homoeopath. But money wasn't everything. Aisling's life was passing her by, and Jenny's behaviour was the last straw. It was high time things began to change.